HIDING EZRA

RITA SIMS QUILLEN

Jan-Carol
Publishing, Inc

"every story needs a book"

HIDING EZRA

Rita Sims Quillen

Published February 2014
Little Creek Books
Imprint of Jan-Carol Publishing, Inc
All rights reserved
Copyright © 2014 by Rita Sims Quillen
Front Cover Illustration: Willard Gayheart
Book Design: Tara Sizemore

ISBN: 9781939289353
Library of Congress Control Number: 2014902529

You may contact the publisher:
Jan-Carol Publishing, Inc
PO Box 701
Johnson City, TN 37605
E-mail: publisher@jancarolpublishing.com
jancarolpublishing.com

To my husband, Mac, and the entire Quillen clan

"One word frees us from all the weight and pain of life:
That word is love."
—Sophocles

LETTER TO READER

Soon after we married, my husband told me the incredible story of his grandfather, Warner Pridemore Quillen, and the trouble he got into during World War I. My husband showed me a tattered journal Warner kept during that time. What an amazing tale! Warner and his family found themselves in this predicament in the midst of the worst pandemic the world had ever seen, the first world war, economic hardship, and some of the coldest weather of their lifetimes. Talk about a harrowing experience! When I began to write poems and stories a few years later, my husband said, "You've got to write a book about Papaw—you're the one to do it."

School, work, children, and life interfered for a long time, but eventually— sometime in the early 1990s—I sat down and wrote the outline of the story that became *Hiding Ezra*. Because I only had a few actual facts regarding Warner's time on the run, the people who had helped him or hunted him, or how he survived, I knew my version would have to be a fictionalized account. Real events inspired me to recreate for you—through imaginary characters, places, and incidents—an unbelievably challenging time in history and in the lives of people like my characters.

I hope that Ezra, Alma, Eva, and Lieutenant Nettles will become some of your favorite characters and that they help you gain a new appreciation for one of the most tumultuous eras in American and Appalachian history.

FOREWORD

Imagine the fragrance of loamy earth freshly turned by a plow, or of a cool damp cellar undisturbed for decades. This sensation of earthiness punctuates the opening sentence of Rita Quillen's novel, even more than the visual image of Ezra flat on his back, almost afraid to breathe, underneath the little country church. Sound also plays large as Ezra listens to the singing of the much-loved hymns and as he strains to hear the voices asking for prayers. These sensory images permeate Quillen's opening scene and lure the reader on to find out why Ezra lies supine under the church, why he longs for familiar voices, why he dares not move till long after the service ends and the people have gone. Though answers to these questions are hinted at, the reason Ezra is hiding comes clear only in bits and pieces as the story unfolds.

Through various authorial devices, Quillen skillfully manipulates the mystery and intrigue surrounding Ezra, his family, and the friends who want to help him. The multiple searches for the elusive protagonist follow a similar pattern, but each one carries its own special victory or defeat, dependent on whether the point of view is that of the prey or the predator. Quillen's use of omniscient point of view allows the reader to meet and know, at least superficially, each of the major characters on both sides of the search; however, she cleverly creates a journal for Ezra to write down his thoughts and actions to keep his "mind occupied and sharp," as he puts it. Thus, his character becomes more fully rounded because we're able to look into his heart, to see his joys, fears, and passions as he records them to remind himself "of what I was and what I am now."

Using her own personal place as the setting for the story, Quillen draws on cultural and geographical characteristics specific to her area. For example, the dialect of her characters accurately depicts that of the Appalachian Mountains, particularly Southwestern Virginia. When Ezra says, "You boys wasn't raised right....You forgot to knock" or "You boys ain't got a bit of manners," the reader familiar with mountain speech feels right at home. Folklore plays a significant role in Ezra's perception of his environment. He studies the number of fogs in August, the heavy coats on the woolly worms, and the squirrels' nut hoards as signs of a hard winter ahead. He takes advantage of a neighborhood legend about a banjo-playing ghost high up in a cave on the mountain. Believing that people will suspect the ghost and will be too scared to investigate, Ezra plays his own banjo at night for the pleasure and good memories the music brings. On one occasion after a refreshing bath in an icy stream, he amuses himself by singing in its entirety a comical folk song about a preacher and a bear. Elements of folklore, oftentimes closely tied to the natural world, make appearances throughout the novel, marking the author as a true recorder of her place.

As important as the culture and terrain of Southwestern Virginia are in this story, Quillen shows the place's connection to the broader world in her revelation of the history of the period, especially hard times brought on by war and disease. She depicts one man's, one family's, one community's plight in a specific time and place, but the reader can easily make the transition from this microcosm to the plight of individuals, families, and communities across the Western world during this era. In her debut novel, Rita Quillen, also an accomplished poet of renown, speaks for the many as she paints a picture of the one. I am hopeful that we will hear this fictional voice again—soon and often.

Grace Toney Edwards, PhD
Professor Emeritus of
Appalachian Studies and English
Radford University
Radford, Virginia

Chapter 1

FALL 1918

Ezra Teague lay flat on his back underneath Wayland Baptist Church, the smell of loam and mint perfuming the air, while the damp earth soaked its coolness into his back. It was one of those clear, cold, crisp mornings when the frosted grass hissed and crackled under his boots, when the sky was unbearably blue and the colors on the hillside were so sharp that it almost hurt to look.

He had traveled there in the dim light just before dawn and waited patiently, napping on and off, until he heard the first thud of horses. Developments in recent days had jangled his nerves: there were fresh tracks of horses and men, plumes of smoke from campfires, occasional gunfire out in the middle of nowhere. It had him spooked, thinking a deputy or soldier was behind every tree. So he thought church was the ideal place to be, even if he couldn't sit inside on the oak pews. It was an especially exciting discovery to find that Wayland Church had a couple of knotholes in some of the floor boards that would allow him not only to hear the service but also to catch a glimpse of the churchgoers.

When the first mournful notes of an old hymn rang out, Ezra closed his eyes and went into the sound, feeling a great sense of peace and contentment, able to forget that he was not inside the church but lying under it like a rat or snake. Preacher Bellamy's voice boomed out a greeting and then began to pray. "We ask your blessing, sweet Lord, on all our boys so far from home in that terrible war and on their families today." Ezra mouthed his own prayer for his friends and neighbors, especially those he had left behind up at Camp Lee, and said "Amen" with the rest of the congregation in the barest whisper.

The congregation then began to offer their special prayer requests and give testimony about themselves or their family's needs. Ezra was always especially interested in this part of the service because it was the only way he could keep up with what was going on. He listened keenly, holding his breath, so he could hear the names of those being discussed. To his astonishment, he heard a female voice he recognized clearly speak from near the front of the church. It was Alma Newton, daughter of former sheriff Samuel Newton, and she was asking for prayer for him and his sister Eva and their entire family in their 'difficulty,' as she put it. Tears welled up in Ezra's eyes because it so touched him that she would do that and because it had been such a long time since he had heard anyone speak his name.

The mood in the congregation did an about-face then, as someone from the back of the church asked for prayer for Roy Dean, and the church laughed loud and long. Ezra pieced together that Roy and his wife Ruby had been engaged in yet another of their frequent fights and that Ruby had run Roy off again, back home to his parents.

To be honest, Ezra thought, *that's really why I like church. More for the people than the sermon.* He felt a little pang of guilt. *What brought me here today isn't hunger for the Word so much as it is for the sound of people laughing, talking, and singing. And because I'm so scared.*

2

Once the sermon and singing were finally over, Ezra kept very still. He listened very hard, barely breathing, to make sure there was no one still around before he even so much as rolled over. He slithered out the back of the church where the brushy undergrowth was thick and slipped over the steep bank down to the creek, where he could walk the rocks back to Hale Springs.

There was an urgent pain in his stomach, and Ezra realized that it was time to find some food. That was the only bad part about this whole mess. Ezra relished solitude, loved roaming the woods. That had always been a primary pastime. But before, he always knew that he could go home and find the dinner that his Mother—or later, his sister Eva—had ready and that there would be a house full of people who loved him that he could talk to. Just then, something moving in the brush startled Ezra so badly that he stumbled and almost fell in the water. Even off-balance, he managed to draw the pistols his father had given him and cock them in a flash. They were his only real possessions now, a .38 and a .32 caliber that he called Father and Son. They were the only family he had now.

The fat groundhog that had caused all the commotion broke through the brush for a second, and, given the close range, Ezra hit it easily with Son. He grinned as he carried the groundhog by the tail back to the cave, thinking *The Lord doth provide*. No more gnawing belly today.

As he fried up the meat, Ezra couldn't stop thinking about the sound of Alma's voice saying his name. It gave him a funny feeling in the pit of his stomach, but then she always seemed to do that. The last time he had seen her was at his mother's funeral. Even in the plain black dress, that silky chestnut hair tied back with a ribbon flashing in the sun, she took his breath. When she turned to smile at someone, he felt a shock go right down into his stomach. She was the most beautiful woman anyone had ever seen. All the boys bid for her attention— a smile, a word from her—all the way through school. And now here she was, thinking about him. He couldn't believe it.

Chapter 2

ALMA FINDS OUT

On the day Alma first heard about Ezra, it was raining so hard and steady that her yard and part of the barnyard had turned into a lake. She imagined Ezra out there, soaking wet and cold, the water coming down so fast and furious that he couldn't even open his eyes. There was news in last week's paper of a deserter from Knoxville being hung; it made Alma's heart leap almost out of her chest to think of it. She rushed onto the porch, ran back in to find a broad-brimmed hat of her father's, went back out on the porch, came back into the house once more looking for a cold biscuit—something Ezra could eat any time—ran back out on the porch, and just sat down on the swing, fighting back tears.

I have no idea where he might be, she thought. *And if I do find him, what do I say? "Hello, I thought I'd bring you this biscuit?"* Alma rubbed her nose and eyes with her sleeve and smiled at her thoughts. *Besides, Joe will be here soon.*

Alma had spent the morning with Mrs. Johnson, the neighbor who had become like a mother to her after she lost her real one, trying different hairstyles and dresses and admiring her handi-work. Her hair was pulled straight back from her face into a tangle of curls at the back. She was wearing a new high-necked cotton dress that her father had ordered from Montgomery Ward for her birthday, but Alma knew Mrs. Johnson had actually picked it out. Her father had invited Joe Stapleton over for dinner. Alma was exasperated at her father's continued attempts to "marry her off," as he called it.

He's buying me all these clothes because he wants me to marry that Stapleton boy. I'll just keep the dresses and lose Joe. Alma thought about how good she looked as she twirled in front of the mirror.

Joe Stapleton was the son of a businessman in town, and he'd been working hard at impressing Sam Newton for several years now. Alma was the catch every young man wanted, but pretty hard to get in the net. The boys generally didn't know what to make of her. The first few that had asked to come see her or offered to go to a church supper with her got scared off pretty quick when they found out she just wasn't like the other girls.

One boy had left and never came back after Alma—on her beautiful gelding, Diamond— challenged him to a race. Another got mad when she had pointed out that he was wrong—Austria was a country, not just a big city in Germany. Of course, the most embarrassing incident, one that had traveled far and wide in the gossip, concerned a young man who made the mistake of being bold enough to try and steal a kiss. Alma told him she wasn't in the mood, but the poor boy had mistaken this for female coyness and the necessary resistance of a 'nice girl' to such attention.. He'd quickly realized his mistake when Alma balled up her fist. She splattered his nose all over his face, and he stomped out of the swept yard, blood squirting through his fingers, yelling for Alma to stay away from him. Alma told people that she didn't really like boys; she told her father, too. Sam worried about it sometimes when she said it. He prayed he hadn't ruined her because he knew her mother would have never forgiven him if he had.

The truth was she loved only one boy. She had always had a crush on Ezra Teague. They didn't see each other often nowadays, but he always made her eyes light up. Alma sometimes wrote his name over and over in the dirt in her flowerbed, daydreamed end-lessly about a wedding—what kind of dress she would wear, who would be invited, the wonderful kiss at the end. She had never told anyone, not her friend Julie, not even Mrs. Johnson who knew all her other secrets. Everyone would try to discourage her, she knew. Ezra was younger that she was, poorer, less educated. Even though her father was not one to look down on people, she knew that he would tell her she could do better.

"How could I possibly do better?" Alma spoke out loud, as she was fastening a loose strand of hair. Even as a little girl, she had loved to see him show up at a community event. On Decoration Day at the cemetery, or the church picnic, even at funerals, Alma would spend a good part of the day sneaking looks at Ezra, trying to watch him without anyone noticing her watching. Not only was he handsome and good-hearted, Ezra could make her laugh, laugh out loud, with tears coming to her eyes. Nobody else could do that.

One of her favorite memories of him was at a church picnic. A crowd of men was gathered around him, swapping tall tales about hunting. Alma pretended to be cleaning up the tables, picking up food scraps for the dogs, so she could get close enough to hear. A woman would not be welcomed or appreciated if she walked over and just sat down in one of these groups, so Alma knew she had to be careful not to be noticed.

Ezra was talking in this Irish accent, retelling a tale his father had told him that his father had told him, and so on. It was something about a man being chased up a tree by a wild pig and the rough bark tore his pants off. Ezra made faces imitating the man, making the sounds of the hog. The men roared and slapped each other on the back as he talked. Another time at a barn-raising, or maybe it was a molasses stir-off, he brought his banjo and played some songs while everyone rested. Alma remembered the children sitting around him in a circle, and he taught them some little rhyming song. It went something like, "Had a little pig, fed him on clover, and when he died, he died all over." Alma giggled at the memory.

When Ezra smiled, Alma realized how rarely people smiled, and he really smiled from somewhere deep inside himself. A person like that is a rare treasure, no matter what his age or what belongings he might have.

Some of her favorite days as a child were those few stolen days she'd had with Ezra. Sometimes when she told her father she was going to Alice's or Helen's, she was actually out with Ezra. He was much more fun that her friends. And he was so different from her father and other boys she knew; Ezra never told her not to do something. He loved to gallop the horses, too, and swing out over the river on a grapevine, and climb the steep, dangerous trail up to the Devil's Bathtub, a beautiful waterfall and swimming hole up in the mountains. Alma's father had said that the Bathtub was too far away and too dangerous for young ladies and had forbidden her from visiting. Alice or Helen would have never done such a thing. *But now he's gone and done something really dangerous,* Alma thought. *This isn't some game. I have to find some way I can help him with this.*

So Alma knew she was not going to marry the Stapleton boy; that was for sure. Her father would be disappointed. *He'll get over it if I make his favorite–custard pie–and hug his neck,* she thought. *And I know how to get rid of Joe Stapleton, too,* she smiled to herself, as she picked up the copy of *Walden* that her aunt had brought her from Kingsport.

When Sam Newton came in that evening, he was thrilled to see Alma and Joe Stapleton sitting together in the swing. He noticed how beautiful Alma looked, how Joe had slicked his hair back and put on a string tie. *I'll not disturb the lovebirds,* Sam thought, *I'll just speak and go on into the house.* But when he stepped up on the porch, he realized that Alma was reading something to Joe from a book and that Joe was looking out across the pasture with a look on his face like he had a bad bellyache. Joe brightened and looked grateful when he saw Sam. He jumped up from the swing and stuck out his hand. "Well, good evening, Mr. Newton. How are you?"

Before Sam could answer, Joe interrupted. "I guess I better go. Now that you're home, I'm sure Alma has things to do and so forth. I better be getting on home."

"Well, do come back as soon as you can, Joe, and we'll keep reading. I'm sure you will be anxious to hear the rest of it." Alma smiled in a way Sam recognized as her 'mischief' smile and he knew she was up to something. "Uh, yeah, sure. See you, Alma." Joe was out across the yard in a flash.

Alma brushed past Sam and started through the door. "If you're hungry, there's some fried potatoes and biscuits on the stove. And I made a custard pie."

Sam knew then that there was no reason to talk about it; Alma had just made up her mind about something and now she was just trying to make him feel better about it. He sighed and followed her through the door. No use trying, he knew. Joe Stapleton was out, too, just like the other two he'd found for her that he thought were good prospects. *At least I get good pies for my efforts,* he thought.

When Sam Newton woke up the next morning, it was still raining a steady drizzle, and the house was quiet. He got dressed, went into the kitchen and poured a cup of coffee, moving silently because he thought Alma had gone back to bed. When he stepped onto the porch, to his surprise Alma was in her riding clothes, sitting in the swing, with that dark look on her face she got when things weren't going her way. He immediately assumed that she was just pouting about the weather and not being able to ride. He stepped out on the porch and made a face at her.

"Your face'll freeze like that."

Alma managed a weak grin at him. "Daddy, did you know about Ezra Teague being in trouble?"

Sam nodded. "I hate it. That family has enough grief with his momma and everything."

"Is there anything we could do?" Alma looked at him anxiously. She leaned forward a little when she said it, even though her hand gripped the chain of the porch swing tightly. She looked as if one word from him would send her in a full run out to the barn, across the field on Diamond's back, and out to rescue the newest of the outlaws, and the realization put a blank look on Sam's face. He said nothing and finally shook his head.

Alma scowled at him, but she let go of the swing and folded her hands in her lap. They were silent for a just a moment, and Sam studied her face from the edge of the porch.

Alma got up and went into the kitchen to warm up the coffee. She left it sitting on the table and went to her room. Stretched out across her bed, she finally dozed off to sleep, dreaming of riding out at full gallop through the woods along Copper Creek, Ezra running out and swinging up on the horse behind her. In another half-dream, half-fantasy, she saw Ezra lying on the ground hurt, and she imagined bringing him back here, putting him in her bed, feeding him soup.

When she woke up, she sat straight up in bed. *I can't bring him back here. All that'll do is get him caught for sure. Ezra will be all right out there, with just a little help.* Alma rubbed the sleep out of her eyes, twisted her hair up into her cap, and pulled it low on her forehead. The rain had stopped, and the air smelled sweet as the morning's laundry. She saddled up Diamond, and they flew across the pasture toward the Teague's place. Eva was about to have an unexpected visitor.

Chapter 3

LIFE ON THE RUN

Lying in the cool shade with his belly full, Ezra drifted off to sleep still thinking of Alma. She was walking toward him, with her hair blowing and her skirt blowing around her legs, showing her bare feet. But then the dream changed, and Ezra saw his mother reaching out to him, handing him bread, and he woke himself, moaning. He sat up to make sure he wouldn't fall asleep again. *Mother. Mother.*

She had suffered so much at the end. Nothing had prepared him for the messy, unbearable reality of watching her die. When the note from Eva had arrived at Camp Lee telling him to come quickly because their mother was very sick, Ezra thought he would come home to find her down with pneumonia or gout and that she would bounce back in a few days, like she always did.

When he walked into her room, with only the single lamp at her bedside table lighting the pitch black, the only pinpoint of light in the little hollow, he saw that his mother had shrunk, her once-beautiful thick hair had turned to little dark wisps like the last fall leaves on the trees. He knew then what Eva hadn't dared tell him in a note.

"Ezra, Ezra." She rasped at him, and he knelt down by her bed, took her hands, the veins dark blue and swollen, and kissed them. He remembered those hands breaking piles of green beans into a huge pot, remembered her standing all morning over a stove, remembered those hands looped through the handle of her coffee cup, remembered her hovering over all ten of them seated at the supper table as they ate like starved pups. Her hair would be curled into little wet ringlets around her face and neck, but she would smile and say, "Y'all go ahead before it gets cold. I believe I'll just have a little buttermilk and cool down."

When Ezra knelt down beside her bed, he could smell the death there, and it made the hair on the back of his neck stand up. "Ezra, you're here. You know what's happening, don't you?" Her eyes burned into his, and she grabbed his shirt collar to pull him closer. "Stay. Eva needs you. Stay. Promise me." Those were the two words he had dreaded hearing.

"I promise." He said it now aloud, in front of his little fire, eating the greasy groundhog, the last dead leaves twisting in the almost-still November air. He had stayed by her side as long as he could. By the time the Army figured out that he wasn't coming back to Camp Lee and sent word by Sheriff Carter that he was now officially AWOL, his mother was long past awareness. He packed up some things and took off into the woods. Eva found only a note, the back door ajar, the smell of his tobacco hanging in the air.

He knew the sheriff wouldn't look for him that hard, anyway. He had told him so.

About ten days before his mother had died, Ezra had been standing on the porch, wishing he could cry, while Eva was inside working with his mother. The sheriff had come riding into the

11

yard. He had some papers in his hand, and the look on his face of one bringing bad news. He motioned Ezra over.

Ezra knew all along this day would come. But he also knew that to have done else would have been unacceptable to him, his family, and his community. He had hoped his mother would be gone before any trouble started. It was a hard place to be in, and he told the sheriff so. Sheriff Carter agreed and squeezed Ezra's shoulder and patted his back before he left. After the sheriff left, Ezra and Eva had packed clothes, blankets, some food, and other supplies into a sack and put it in the smokehouse.

Ezra stayed one more day to say goodbye to his mother, then slipped off in the night so Eva wouldn't have to watch him go. In just a few days, his mother passed on, and Ezra found himself having to watch the funeral hidden in a rhododendron thicket a little way up the mountain, watching and crying, flat on his belly, as his mother's coffin was lowered in the ground. He could barely hear Psalm 121—his mother's favorite—read over her, as family and neighbors huddled around Eva and his brothers. Ezra stared hard into Eva's back, hoping she could feel his presence and know how sorry he was that he wasn't down there with his arm around her, too.

STARTING HIS JOURNAL— THOSE FIRST DAYS

Two weeks after his mother's death, Ezra was still running from rock to rock, tree to tree, until he was high on Stone Mountain in the stiff autumn wind. He was sure he would be caught at any moment. His heart beat very fast and wouldn't slow down even when he stopped to rest, and his hands and legs had a tremble in them. After two days, he was starved and exhausted.

I can't go on like this, he thought. *I have to eat. I have to have shelter. If I can make it for just a few weeks, they'll get tired of looking for me. They'll have to go back. There's a lot of work to do in the army.*

Ezra had crept down from his safe peak to a valley where there were some farmhouses. He waited until nightfall and then stole a couple of eggs and a pumpkin from Tom Smith's garden. Then he went home and slipped in the old storage shed behind the house where he had stashed some of his hunting and fishing gear. Ezra was delighted to see how useful these items would be in his present circumstances; there was a lantern, an iron skillet, some fishing line and hooks, an old ratty blanket and some matches. He left Eva a note telling her he was all right and to bring some things to him at Hale Springs Cave.

This'll just be like a good, long hunting trip, he thought. *I just have to make a month or so, maybe two. That won't be that bad. I've just got to keep my head.*

The walk to the springs that first time was a long one, and the hunger made Ezra weak and lightheaded. As soon as he was down in a little swag where the smoke wouldn't be noticeable, he built a fire and fried his eggs as best he could. Without fat they stuck to the skillet pretty bad and he didn't get but a few bites out of them. He then scooped out the inside of the pumpkin and cooked it. With no sugar or butter or salt, the sharp-tasting mush wasn't very appetizing, but Ezra knew he couldn't be too picky at this point.

This is it, he thought. *This is my new life. If I'm gonna live like this, I've got to start using my head. I better get busy figuring some things out.*

So Ezra hiked to a high rock and sat there all day, pondering things. His first thought was to try to plan some way to get out of here. There were now trains rolling in two directions through the county—one went back and forth between Elkhorn City, Kentucky, and Spartanburg, South Carolina; the other made a much shorter run from Appalachia, Virginia, over in the coalfields to Bristol. *I never been to Spartanburg or Elkhorn City. Nobody notices a stranger in towns that big*, he thought. There were ferries up and down the Holston, too, that he could catch over in Kingsport and ride way down into Tennessee. But then he saw Eva's face, and his father sitting by the window, and the face of Sheriff Carter. *They'll expect me to try to run, and they'll be watching.* Ezra knew he was going to have to think of a better plan.

The first thought that came to him was that he had to find shelter. When he penned Eva's note telling her to bring things to the Hales Springs Cave, he was just thinking of a drop-off point out of the weather, but it now occurred to him that there was no reason he couldn't sleep in there, too. Sleeping out in the open was just too nerve-wracking. He felt too vulnerable and exposed. On his second night on the run, he'd woke up and nearly died of fright when a large dog had been standing practically on top of him, smelling of his arm.

The caves across the creek from the Hale Springs had been favorite places in his boyhood. They weren't very big; he couldn't stand up in there. But he could definitely sleep and sit in there, in a place that was fairly dry as well as cool in the summer and warmer in the winter. The cave would have to do for now. And there was a tunnel there through a narrow part of the ridge that old man Hale had dug. Like God himself, old man Hale had turned Copper Creek in a new direction, to make the water run his mills.

Thinking to sneak it to Eva, Ezra made a new list of things. But then he ran out of paper and broke the little piece of a pencil he had. He took a long route back to the house to leave the note. It was dark when he crossed the hill and saw the Midway school-house. He watched it for a while to make sure nobody was around. Then he ran to the back of the building and raised the window. In a minute he was inside, blasted in the face with that schoolhouse smell he'd forgotten.

The sound of Ezra's heavy footsteps echoed in the room, and he flinched like someone might hear him. He walked up to the front of the room and sat at Miss Fletcher's desk. There were two good pencils lying there, and he took both of them. There was a notebook, too, with some writing in it. Ezra removed the pages that were written on and laid them on the desk. He remembered that he had some change in his pocket, so he left Miss Fletcher a dime for the pencils and paper. He wondered what Miss Fletcher would think. It made him smile to himself to think of the puzzlement she'd feel. Probably nobody had heard yet about him running away; even if she had, she probably wouldn't dream for a minute that Ezra was the mysterious visitor who stole her pencils. *What would an outlaw want with pencils and paper, anyway?*

That thought took the smile right off his face. He was an outlaw. It was the first time that had occurred to him. Ezra groaned aloud and covered his face with his hand. *How did I get in such a mess? I'm so glad Momma isn't around to see this. Eva must be worried to death. Lord, forgive me, I didn't mean for this to happen.*

Ezra stopped with one leg out the window and looked back into the room. He looked back at the desk where he used to sit and tried to remember how it had felt then to be young and carefree. Then in one fluid motion, he was on the ground, the window shut behind him, and he ran off across the little clearing, clutching his new treasure.

He napped underneath some laurel until about dusk and then set out walking toward the cave. He was pleased to find it just as he remembered, only better: the opening of the cave was covered over with brush, and the top of a dogwood tree growing up from the creek bank provided even more cover. *This is much better,* he thought, and crawled back into the deepening darkness. He curled himself into a ball, like one of Eva's cats, and slept for several hours.

Ezra woke to the dreamed words of his sister, "Ezra, time to get up. Biscuits are almost done." He sat up, grabbed his pencils and notebook, and moved into the sun to try to warm up. Keeping his head and upper body in the shade, safely hidden from view by the branches of the dogwood, he propped his legs up on a rock in the sun, and immediately he felt a little tiny bit more warmth. He beat on his legs and feet with his fists and wiggled them around.

When he felt better and more awake, he took his homemade pole and one of his granddaddy's old fishing lures down to the creek and caught a little baby trout in just a few minutes. *Things is gonna go my way today. I'm gonna be able to get this fried up good before the fog lifts so there's no chance of being seen.*

When there was nothing left of the little fish but a pile of tiny bones at this side, Ezra took out his pencils and the notebook and began to write. *This will keep my mind occupied and sharp,* he said to himself. *And it will help me remember stuff later.* He had to sit and think several minutes to figure out what day it was and to decide what he wanted to write. *Crawling around on my belly, not being at my own mother's funeral, what a sad, sorry mess I'm into. That's what I got to write about.* Here he was eating on a cold fall morning, alone, an outcast, a wanted man, trying to pass the time and keep his wits sharp, all his days like a Sunday afternoon, much calmer now than when he had first run away. He reached into his pack and pulled out his little folder and began to write.

Oct. 10, 1918

Hello book. I am going to write to you every day so I can remember things later and so I won't forget how. When you are by yourself all the time with no one to talk to, your mind could get rusty. They talked to us about it at Camp Lee about what could happen if you get captured and wind up in one of them prison of war camps. They said that the only ones who come out of it pretty well are the ones who keep their mind occupied and don't let things get to them so bad. So I'm gonna write down what I do every day, the weather, memories of good times, my prayers. I can remind myself of what I was and what I am now.

I know a lot of people will wonder about me because of this. They'll say I'm some kind of chicken, call me a weakling or a momma's boy. It hurts me to think of it. It hurts me even more to think that people might say so to Eva or some of the rest of the family. I hope that most people will know me better than that. They know I'm a hard worker and I've never been one to run from a fight or from trouble if something had to be done. Times is just so hard for us right now.

I can't see that government making me go clear across the ocean to fight about something I don't really understand when my mother and daddy was both sick and so much work to be done just to survive. And on top of that, everybody's sick and dying with this terrible flu. I heard one of the officers at Camp Lee talking to another officer, telling him that the flu was killing more of our men than the Kaiser's men ever would. What if Eva was to get that flu while I was over across the water somewheres, not even knowing what was going on? Who would take care of daddy? The Army will forget about me, and I can get back to doing what I need to do.

Oct. 12, 1918

I walk the high ridge cliff over Copper Creek, hanging in the skyline over the river. It's a little risky, no, it's a lot risky. But I cannot abide the skulking around behind trees and rocks today. I want to feel the wind. I want to climb the rocky path across the hill, pass under the big twisted oak that always reminds me of the Tree of Life, down by Joe Harper's throbbing hum of bees. I'll stomp right through matted briers and chiggerweeds and imagine the smell of that honeysuckle and wild rose. I will lift up mine eyes unto these hills from whence cometh my help.

Oct. 19, 1918

Hale Springs—I have always been drawn to water. That's why, even in this most awful time of my life, I'm here close to it. As a boy I loved rain, loved to see it fill up the pockets in our dirt yard with pools brown as chestnuts. The other kids would scream and run inside when it stormed, but not me.

I would hurry out and drop flat to the ground, let that rain pellet my face like bird shot. I loved to sneak off and go swimming in the Clinch. You see a lot of wildlife near water. Once I saw a shy doe with twins come to the water. And those huge cranes would rise up dragging those long, long legs. When Eva and me was little, we'd come here at the springs to wade. She loved the little purple flowers and the little mussel shells. She would wade in up to her knees, trying to pinch the tadpoles in her little fat fingers. I can still see those big sad eyes when she'd look to me for sympathy when they got away.

Oct. 21, 1918

The only good thing I can see about this whole mess is that I've finally been able to do as much hunting as I want to. I love to hunt, always have, ever since I's a boy. I love the smell of the black dirt on the floor in the deep woods, that wet dirt smell, and all the other smells, too. A lot of times you can smell the animals and such, too, that cucumber smell that copperheads have, and that strong smell of deer, especially during the rut. I love tracking and trying to outsmart the animals, deer and turkey especially. That's what I been going after today. I seen a hen and a gang of younger ones and trailed them all the way up Barker Knob but never did see no tom. That's what I'm wanting, a big old fat tom turkey that I can sneak down to Eva for a Sunday dinner surprise fit for a queen.

Oct. 24, 1918

I watched a hog killing today, and it was one of the funniest things I ever saw in my life. It was down at the Starnes. The family carried old man Starnes out in the yard and set him in a chair to watch. That littlest boy of theirs, I can't think of his name, pitched a fit to be the one to shoot the hog. Jake handed him the pistol, and he raised it up and aimed a long time, but he still just about missed that hog. That's the worst thing that can happen——end up with a wounded hog.

That big sow went plumb crazy and started chasing all of them around the yard. People was flying in all directions. Some of the kids shimmied up a big plum tree and climbed out on to the roof of the smokehouse, squealing and hollering up a storm. The women broke for the house. That left the pig and old man Starnes alone in the yard, and he was yelling "Holy hell!" and "God hep us!" and that pig turned his chair a flip. I had to put my hands over my mouth, I swear, I was laughing so hard, but I felt bad about it 'cause the old man coulda been hurt. That pig even run up on the porch and into the house until it came flying back out, with one of the women right after it. The funniest thing of all about it is that about that time, the oldest boy put one clean shot thru that hog's neck, and it fell over deader than a hammer. They all just come back out into the yard, real slow and serious, got the old man righted in his chair, started cleaning that hog just like nothing had happened. It beat anything I ever saw.

Oct. 28, 1918

I guess I ought to put down some thoughts on the Army while it's still fresh in my mind. I met lots of good folks there. A lot of them were from right around here somewhere, but I didn't know them before we got called up. I met some I didn't care for, too. But I don't dwell on that. There was lots of things about the Army I liked. We was outside a lot, and they had us do a lot of shooting, which a lot of us were already pretty good at, and running these things called obstacle courses.

That was one of the things about the Army that didn't make a whole lot of sense. They'd make us get up before daylight to get started making everything clean and neat. I always thought Momma was pretty particular, but in the army she'd be sent to scrub the latrines. That's what they made you do if you got on their bad side for any reason. Anyway, they made us scrub the bathrooms with little tiny brushes, check for dust and lint under our bunks, even up in the springs. If we left a wrinkle the size of a hair in our bunk when we made it up, we were gonna get yelled at.

We had to bathe and shave every day, and we had to keep our boots so shiny we could use them for mirrors—then they'd send us for a long hike or out on that obstacle course. I just scratched my head about a lot of things in the Army.

Nov. 12, 1918

I wish I was back at Camp Lee. Everybody was sad about me going in the Army, and some fellows I talked to said I was heading straight to hell. But I kind of like it. I got to know some fine people there. The food wasn't bad, and they had some fine weapons. I even liked the training, the rope climbing and the obstacle courses. A man needs a test ever now and then. He needs to know how he stacks up.

I done all right for myself. I was proud of my shooting up there. Pa would've grinned like a mule eating sawbriers if he'd seen me put nine out of ten shots right in that bullseye like I did. I woulda been a good soldier, I think, but I guess I'll never know now. Ain't no way the Army would have me back now.

Rocks

I never noticed rocks before. They were just an aggravation, in the way when you plowed or when you tried to get down the road. But now I notice the different colors. I didn't know God said brown and gray in so many different ways. Being inside the cave is like being inside a stone. It's cold and dark in way that is different from outside cold and dark. I worry that I am becoming hard and cold, that this time in the woods living like an animal will turn my heart to stone, my soul into gravel. The only sound tonight is my breath and the rain outside. I lay awake thankful for the shelter of the cave, amazed by the wall of water upon the earth. It seems like a solid curtain. I wonder about the crops and how Eva is doing with them. Our tobacco will be early this year because of all the rain. It's been cut now, but I worry about Eva having to finish and get it to market all by herself. I had a great idea yesterday, and I spent today checking it out. There's a cave across Copper Creek near the Foam Hole that I used to love to go in when I's a kid. It's called the Rock House. I just got to thinking that would be a place to hide out of the weather, but I really wasn't sure how big it was. When you're little, everything seems bigger to you than when you're an adult. Anyway, I went over there. I was tickled to find that even though it's not that big, I can still get in and out of it all right. When you go in you have to crawl on your hands and knees, but then you can straighten up into this little room. It'll make a pretty good little hideout. But that's not really the great idea.

What I remembered is that a lot of people think there's a ghost up there, old man Hale, the banjo-playing ghost. I can't remember all the details of the story, but I think he was killed in the War Between the States. People say that at night, walking by the old place on the way to the springs, you can hear the banjo music. Jake Starnes says that the ghost was rolling stones down the hill in front of him one time, swore to it. He said he walking over through there about dark and that every little bit along that path a stone or two would roll down the hill in front of him. He said there's no way that it would just be an accident. I don't know about it, I been through there lots of times, and I ain't never seen or heard nothing. But a lot of folks won't go through there at night for nothing. See, if I get Eva to bring me my banjo up here, I can play it some at night in the cave, and if anybody hears me, they will think it's the ghost, and they will run away and not come back. I am sure feeling good to think that I could get to play my banjo some. People will just think that something has got that old ghost stirred up again.

November 1918

It's blue cold today. My moustache is froze hard and cutting my lower lip. The signs were right. Eight heavy fogs in August—that means a lot of snows this winter. And the squirrels over on Stock Creek hoarding nuts that away, the long coat on those woolly worms. I've never seen more sign of hard times. I'll have to find Eva plenty of firewood. It'll warm us twice—once in the getting and once in the burning. This will be the forever and ever winter.

Winter 1918

I can't get over Alma saying my name like that in church. She ought not to have done it. I've always been sweet on her. There's no other girls around here like her. She always smiled at me, and I kind of flirted with her a time or two, but I was real careful what I said to her. She's a fine lady and the apple of her daddy's eye, that's for sure. Just think what it would be like to have a wife like Alma. I think about that a lot of the time now.

There's a lot of things I'd like to do with her. I'd like to ride with her. I've just got old Annie and daddy's old mare, and Alma's got that fine, fine paint her daddy bought for her, but she don't care about that. She'd ride slow so I could keep up, I know she would. I'd like to take her up in that meadow across Copper Creek. I bet she's never been there. I'd take one of Eva's quilts and let her lay on it while I picked blackberries and fed them to her.

And I'd like to take her bird hunting with me. I do have a good bird dog, Joe, and I bet she could shoot a quail over him. Her daddy taught her to shoot pretty good, I hear. I was just thinking that Alma is different from any woman I ever knowed around here. She always smells really good, like honeysuckle, every time I've ever been around her, even when we were kids. And she has some pretty clothes. But then, I've seen her out on that horse with pants and a hat on and boots, and I swear, she acts like a boy. In them boots, she even walks with her feet apart kindly and moves her shoulders. I don't know—it's strange.

EVA'S VIGIL

Eva's day started around 5 am every morning. She lifted the covers and stepped into the cold dark and onto the rough plank floor, grabbed her clothes off the chair, and jumped back under the covers to change in the warm tent of her bedding. First task was to get the fire in the pot-bellied stove blazing hot again, and then she built the fire in the cookstove. As soon as the coffee started boiling, the smell would wake her father. Eva would help him out of bed and get him comfortable wrapped up near the stove before she even started breakfast.

In the first days after Ezra left, Eva would fly onto the porch and then to the smokehouse every morning to see if Ezra might have come back or at least left some note or sign that he'd been there. Her bundle she'd left in the smokehouse contained beef jerky they'd made last year, two pencils, a dollar from her egg money, some warm clothes, and a drawing she'd done of her mother. On the sixth morning, Eva was thrilled to find the bundle gone. She leaned in the door of the smokehouse and wept. Ezra was all right.

Some days her fatigue and worry would almost get the best of her. She paced the floor like a hound about to give birth, moving continuously from the front door to the back door to the window. A few times she put on a sweater and hat and started out the door to go look for Ezra, but she always came to her senses and stopped. *If I go look for him, somebody might be following me and I'll lead them right to him,* she thought. *The sheriff told me after the funeral that we need to convince Ezra to come in and do the right thing. He thinks we're scared of the law.*

By the time Ezra had been gone a month, a numb sadness had settled over Eva. She still couldn't believe that her mother was gone; occasionally, she would think to herself, *I'll have to ask Momma this or I need to tell Momma that* and then remember.

Eva's father's stroke had taken his voice, so with her mother and brother gone, Eva's world fell silent except for the purring of her cat or the soft bellowing of the calf in the pasture. She began to talk to herself out loud, discussing the memory of how her mother made sweet-potato pie or what kind of flower seed she'd like to order for spring. Her father sat by the stove all day or at the window and slept mostly. Sometimes when she was talking, he would look at her as if he were listening. Eva was most content on those days, when he seemed to be back among them. Sometimes she would catch him looking at her, and her mind would flash back ten years to when he and her mother were younger and vigorous and several of the children were still at home. Her daddy would "tell his big tales," as her momma always put it, about when he was young, about hunting and fishing, about haunted houses, and the ache of longing and loss would so overcome her that she would get up and stand with her back to him so he couldn't see her cry.

The only thing that brought her any peace and joy now was her quilts. Eva was a master with needle and cloth; that's what Ezra always said. From the time she was a little girl, Eva was the artistic one in the family. She could just look at anything and draw it. Her daddy used to call it "scribbling away money" and told her she used up more paper than anybody he ever saw except for that crooked lawyer in Gate City. He would say it in a gruff voice like he was fussing, but his eyes were grinning, and Eva knew he was actually proud of her talent.

During the years when she got to go to school, Eva would make posters for the schoolroom walls for each holiday. The proudest day of her life was the day she won the God Bless America contest the school system sponsored. She was so nervous and excited to walk into Shoemaker College and see the posters that children from all over the county had submitted all down the hallway walls. When she got to the auditorium and saw all the people, Eva felt like she would throw up, but then she saw her poster on an easel at the front of the room. They had her come up front and accept her prize—a blue ribbon and a silver dollar! Eva had her picture taken with her principal and Mr. Richmond, the hardware store owner in town who had sponsored the contest. The picture appeared in the local paper that week, and Eva's mother cut it out and taped it near the kitchen window. The poster was still hanging in Eva's bedroom, and the newspaper cutting was carefully folded into the big family Bible.

The reverie prompted Eva to get out some paper and pencils. She was deep into a drawing of her father in his younger days, plowing with his old mule, when Alma Newton rode into the yard looking like one of the beautiful princesses in the picture books at school. Eva thought about hiding and pretending she wasn't home. She looked down at the faded dress and the apron with a hole in it and cringed. But there was no time to set anything right. Alma was on the porch and knocking on the door. Eva opened the door just a crack and tried to say "Hello," but her voice cracked because she hadn't spoken all day.

"I'd like to talk to you if you have a minute. I think you know what it's about."

Eva finally managed to whisper out, "Come on in."

The two women sat in rockers near the fireplace and just smiled and exchanged pleasantries for a few minutes. Alma was taking in every detail of the sparsely furnished room. She made sure her eyes didn't reveal her shock at seeing Eva's frail father propped up on pillows in a chair in the corner. He seemed to be asleep, oblivious to everything. *Poor, poor Eva. How hard and lonely this is. I'm alone taking care of my father, too, but it's nothing like this.*

"I wanted to know if there's anything I can do, Eva. Daddy, too. We want to help. I'm really, really sorry about your mother. I know a little bit about how hard that is."

Eva felt the tears welling up and her face turned red at the thought of crying in front of Alma, someone she didn't know well, someone who everyone held in reverence. But she couldn't stop. Alma was the first woman to come comfort her, and something tender in her voice reminded Eva of the ache of longing she carried for her mother and of her father, whose voice was gone forever, and of Ezra, who was somewhere out there with no one to talk to either, and she began to shake silently as the tears rolled down her face.

Alma didn't know what else to do but to go over and put an arm around Eva and let her lean on her.

"I want to help Ezra, too, Eva. There must be something I can do to help."

"Well, maybe there is." Eva wiped her face on her sleeve and began to tell her everything- about how Ezra was hiding in the Rock House, about people leaving food for him in outbuildings. Alma just listened intently, saying nothing, revealing nothing, until Eva told her about riding out to Hale Springs to what everyone called the Foam Hole on Copper Creek and leaving notes and supplies for him. Alma grinned and then, to Eva's surprise, threw her head back and laughed out loud.

Chapter 5

LIEUTENANT NETTLES' MISSION

Andrew Nettles grew up on a quiet street in Big Stone Gap, in southwest Virginia, not too far from Ezra Teague's Scott County home. His father had been a successful businessman, owning a hardware store in town. His mother, Roberta Arnott Nettles, was the only daughter of one of the town's old families who "had money," people said. In truth, they didn't have much money, but they had property and status and pretensions. Roberta's mother had insisted on dressing for dinner, always wearing a hat whenever she went out, having ladies over for a book club luncheon—all things her mother had told her went on every day in the world outside "these hills."

The Arnott family had come to Big Stone Gap when almost everyone else had: during the coalmining, railroad-building days in the 1880s. Stories still circulated in the local lore about Roberta's mother, whom everyone referred to as 'Miz Stella,' getting off the train, in a beautiful burgundy silk dress and a hat with a big feather, with 10 trunks of clothes and household items loaded on wagons.

Miz Stella never completely adjusted to the mud, the gray fortress of hills around her, the roughness of her Big Stone Gap neighbors. While her husband Jacob worked in the railroad office, she ran their home like a business and raised her children with one purpose: to persuade them to leave the godforsaken place and make something of themselves. She punished any hint of a mountain accent in their speech, visibly shuttered if they used words like 'recollect' for 'remember' or 'hit' for 'it.' But to her bitter disappointment, it didn't work. Roberta, her pride and joy, fell in love with a smooth-talking, handsome local boy named Jimmy Nettles and settled into a house right down the street. Jimmy was one of those mountain men for whom words were currency. He was a storyteller extraordinaire, his talk vivid and imaginative and original. Roberta was as spellbound by him as was everyone else, and soon her own speech was sprinkled with his imagery and colorful similes. When Roberta told one of her friends to stop "grinnin' like a mule eatin' sawbriers" about something, Miz Stella frowned. When Roberta complained that her mother's chicken dinner was "tough as whit leather," the double insult was too much, and Miz Stella took to her bed with a sick headache for three days. After Roberta and Jimmy ran off and got married, her mother never completely recovered and never forgave Roberta for her treachery.

So Andrew was born into a house of confusion and conflict. From the time he was little, there were all these strange rules, mixed messages, and unspoken tensions in the grownup world around him. "Yes, Andrew, you can play on this street and visit this house; No, Andrew, we don't go over there." He could visit some churches with his friends (one of the few acceptable social activities) but not others.

His father had lots of friends of all kinds, from the local circuit court judge to the local Coonhunter Club members with their baying hounds. Jimmy Nettles never saw a stranger. Andrew loved to go into the yard and listen to the men talk about their hunting trips or tell stories about when they were little. Early on, he noticed that his mother and father talked very differently from each other and had different friends and different interests. Although Roberta never grew as extreme on the issue as her mother, nevertheless, as she got older she became more like her; it was apparent that she had high expectations of her son, and these included getting an education and moving far beyond what she saw as the confines of Big Stone Gap. As a teenager, old enough to begin to ponder the mysteries of love and women and marriage, he grew more and more confused about his parents' apparent mismatch. They obviously cared about one another very much; they never fought or spoke cruelly to each other. But they sometimes looked at each other with sadness—sadness that Andrew became part of. It attached itself to his face and hung there almost all the time.

Somehow, the feeling of being better than everyone, which he had inherited from his mother, and the feeling of inferiority that his uneducated father had passed on mixed into a strange demeanor and personality that limited him in his career in the military. Everyone at Camp Lee and at Camp Oglethorpe where he had been stationed before knew of his limitations, too. To put it mildly, people had a strong reaction to him, mostly negative. So he knew that number three in command was probably as high as he was going to get. At times he knew; other times he fantasized about being first in command.

When he heard about the Teague desertion, one of several that spring at Fort Lee, he saw it simply as an opportunity. If he could solve this embarrassing problem for the Army, they would be very grateful. There was quite a bit of discussion among the higher-ups about the sizeable number of AWOL soldiers, and the government had a dilemma. If they made too much of it, the publicity might just encourage more to refuse to do their duty. On the other hand, it would hard to find these men without publicizing the issue. The military couldn't afford to be wasting a lot of man-power with a war on. Nettles had decided to take the matter into his own capable hands; he walked into the commander's office and volunteered to spearhead the effort to solve this problem. Several officers had come by later to talk to him, shake his hand, and wish him luck. They seemed relieved, very relieved, in fact. Nettles knew why now.

That morning, two of the duller recruits he had trained in an earlier group appeared in his office. Smith and Cooper were two of the slowest country boys to ever fall off the pumpkin truck. They were from somewhere down in coal country; most people couldn't understand half of what they said. When they told him they had been assigned to his 'retrieval detail,' as they called it, Nettles stood up and looked out the window so they couldn't see his face.

"We're gonna hep you find this Teague feller and maybe a couple of them others from down 'at way," Smith said, and Cooper nodded in agreement. "We're lookin' forward to it."

Nettles just looked at them. *If these are the type of yokels that I'm to be saddled with on this assignment, these runaways are home free. Why doesn't the brass realize that I need some good people? This Teague fellow is no fool, and he's on his home turf.* Nettles remembered him from basic. He was tough, strong, an excellent marksman. *These rubes couldn't find an old lady's cat.*

All he said to the two men was, "Good. You'll be leaving tomorrow morning. See the quartermaster for your supplies. I'll have detailed directions and instructions ready for you then. Dismissed."

"You mean," Cooper stopped and frowned. "You ain't a-goin' sir?"

"No, Private. I've got too much to do here. We've got inspections in a few weeks. You should be able to handle this on your own. Is there anything else, Private?" Nettles gave them his best dead stare.

"No sir." They were out the door in a second.

Nettles knew that the odds were against them, but at least, the strike-out would be on their records, not his. If the top brass thought they were going to saddle him with boobs like that and get away with it, they better think again. They'll reconsider and send some real soldiers, men of substance, when these come back empty-handed. *And I'll be the hero, not the clown,* Nettles smiled to himself.

Chapter 6

COMMUNITY
REACTION

The old men who gathered down at Blevins Store were the first to hear news of Ezra Teague's situation, and they told their wives about it. As folks would visit church revivals or family dinners, they would hear the talk of the man living on the run in the woods, all because he had stayed home with his dying mother. Most of the women had sympathy and saw Ezra as yet another reason why this war business was so wrong.

The winter of 1918-1919 was an anxious time for everyone in America. Almost everyone had a loved one, friend, or acquaintance who got on the train with one of the two big groups that had been called up to Camp Lee. The war was like the sun, moon, planets—something so far away, so big, that people really couldn't get their minds around it. They had heard tales of wartime from their parents and grandparents, but the War Between the States was nothing like this. As bad as that war was, at least it was here. The battlefields—and more importantly, the graves—could be visited.

But the idea of going off to war cross the ocean was so scary as to be unimaginable. The last thoughts before sleep of many wives and mothers concerned the possibility of their loved one injured or dying alone on some foreign soil with no one to understand their last words, maybe no one to even read a little scripture.

Any war news, even if it was bad, was gold, and traffic in Blevins' store had grown significantly. There was one local weekly newspaper in the county, and the closest town of any size, Kingsport, Tennessee, had a daily paper. People who could read and afford a newspaper grabbed them off the stands, looking for the war news first. But most relied on word-of-mouth passed along. They would come by the store just to hear the news.

Controversy continued to swirl around the new mandatory military service. As the war dragged on, the thousands died from the flu here on American soil; the toll on soldiers in the field from the new horrible weapon called mustard gas grew, too. Local draft boards, formed all over the country to oversee a fair implementation of the new Selective Service Act, found themselves swamped with applications for exemption.

The old men who sat around the checkerboard still had collective memory of the forced conscriptions of the Civil War era and were generally supportive of some young men's reluctance to serve. A few of the men, though, saw Ezra as a coward, hiding behind his mother's skirts in wartime. Some of the men got into a heated argument over Ezra's situation and the war in general.

"A man's got a duty to his country," one man said. "If he had really only wanted to stay with his mother a while, not shirk his duty in wartime, he could have asked from some time off."

"What do you know about it?" another said. "It ain't right, what they're doin'. Callin' every man in the county except the old men and little boys to go off, when times is this hard."

Joe Blevins tried to stay out of these arguments since he was on the local draft board that had been set up to hear appeals from those who didn't think they could or should serve. It was the worst thing that had ever happened to him; there were dark circles under his eyes and his apron hung looser around his waist from the strain of the worry and the sleepless nights. These folks were his neighbors and, he had to admit it, his customers. If everyone got mad at him, his business could suffer.

Government and military officials were shocked and outraged to learn that in many localities, particularly in rural areas, a majority of the white men with the temerity to ask to be excused were receiving their wish from the local draft board. Down in Fulton County, Georgia, 526 of the 818 white men who applied were exempted, local papers reported. Selective Service officials dismissed the whole board. But the problem wasn't confined to one area or region. It was widespread.

The government pressed local officials to arrest these known deserters, but local sheriffs found that any attempt to round up and prosecute these men was extremely unpopular in many locales. Unwilling to sacrifice their own political careers, they simply 'played both sides,' putting up a pretense of cooperating with government and military officials but actually expending very little effort to find and arrest the AWOL soldiers.

Blevins felt he had to speak up against the Teague boy, though his heart did go out to him. He knew he couldn't publicly condone desertion and have any credibility with either the public or his fellow Draft Board members.

Blevins cleared his throat and stepped around the end of the counter closer to the checker players. "If the Teague boy had come to us, he could have convinced the board to give him one of them deferrals, the Army calls them, and he could have reported for duty later. He's gone about this in the wrong way."

"But his mother didn't get so bad until he was already gone. It was too late." One of the men said. "Besides, everybody's heard about how they did up in Abingdon. Up there, only the big shots and people who owned a lot of land got them deferrals you're talking about. The poor boys had to go, them that wasn't nobody, come hell or high water."

Blevins' face reddened a little. "That wouldn't happen here." He stopped rubbing the counter and looked hard at the group.

"Well, I ain't saying that it would, Joe, but I'm just saying Teague woulda heard about it and about all the men who've run off. He sure ain't the only one. They's two down in Duffield that they've been lookin' for now for about two months."

Blevins just shrugged and started emptying sacks of coffee. The men let it go then and went back to playing checkers.

For the most part, however, folks didn't think much one way or another about the deserters. They were too busy working tobacco or trying to keep enough firewood in. On top of everything else, the constant labor strife in the coalfields was leading to an increasing problem with the coal supply. There was really more to worry about than anyone could grasp all at once. There was so much trouble of every kind and description that people lived with a knot of fear and nervousness inside that never went away.

Mrs. Blevins had taken to staying in the back of the store, and some days Joe could tell she'd been crying. She was worrying some over the war, although no one from their immediate family was called up. The major reason for her tears was the sickness. A friend and a cousin had already died of the flu. She was terrified that all the people coming in and out of the store would carry the plague to them. Joe was scared, too, but he had to keep the store open, and somebody had to go out and wait on these people.

As the war dragged on, so did the controversy, and the federal government found itself with a worsening problem on its hands. The papers almost always mentioned something about the defections and the resistance to the draft, about the attempts at escape from the worst of the military installations, such as Camp Oglethorpe, where thousands died from the flu. An unwilling army is probably not going to be a successful army; an army that's too small is certain to fail. They had to have soldiers, but they also had to try and keep as much public goodwill as possible. In the case of the Ezra Teague, the Army certainly didn't publicize their search because they feared that it would backfire. It would possibly cause hostile feeling toward the military from a local population already inclined to mistrust and fear the government, and it might even inspire a lot more copycat defections. There was already enough of a problem in that regard.

When the Army folks came into the area looking for some of the AWOL soldiers, they tried to keep a very low profile. Smith and Cooper, Nettles' men, did make some homemade posters with a description of Teague, asking people to contact Sheriff Carter if they saw him. Most of the time, someone would tear the posters down off of trees and fence posts as they went by, not because they were concerned about Teague necessarily, but just because they knew it would be an embarrassment to the family. The fact that tearing down the posters might annoy 'the gov'mint' wasn't lost on them, either.

When soldiers first showed up in the county, there was lot of talk about them. Locals had heard that the Germans were sending spies over here to try to do whatever they could to help their cause. Local officials had even begun to post guards at bridges in strategic areas asking for identification from people they didn't know. "How do we know these aren't German spies, dressed up in stolen uniforms, speaking perfect English to fool us?" people said. Sheriff Carter checked up on them, just in case, and was able to reassure people that they were indeed who they said they were.

But that wasn't much comfort. The idea of a group of soldiers running around spying on people in hopes of catching Ezra did not sit well with the residents. Motives were not as important as the issue of spies and outsiders in their midst.

The fact that the Army men came and went caused confusion and suspicion, too. Because there were others they were hunting in addition to Ezra, the detail would occasionally leave the search for Ezra to venture into other communities in search of other errant soldiers. They had better luck in several of those cases, locating the men in question, and for a while, the Army tried to be lenient with the runaways, convincing them to return to Camp Lee, promising them light punishment and reinstatement if they came willingly.

By the fall of 1918, the military became much more aggressive in their pursuit of those who had gone AWOL or who had refused to cooperate in the draft process in their home localities. In November, the military prosecuted its first deserters for treason—two Georgia men—and hanged them.

When the Army details searching for the other two Scott County deserters would leave the area, the community breathed a sigh of relief—but was even more unnerved and shaken when the soldiers reappeared yet again. It was like thinking an epidemic was over, only to discover more dead and dying.

The people also had a personal reaction to the Army men looking for Ezra, Smith and Cooper. The men in the detail—especially the younger one, Cooper, who folks called 'Curly' because of his wild hair—were not Southerners and had that loud brashness that so grated on the mild manners of Ezra's neighbors. The men down at the store had a very blunt message for Smith and Cooper when they first began asking questions about Teague's whereabouts.

It was a usual Saturday evening outside the store, with the usual gang gathered to talk and laugh and swap stories. Jeb Flanary always brought his banjo, and some of the young boys were dancing around kicking up a curtain of white dust and squalling out "Whooeee!" just as the Army detail rode right up close to them and dismounted in the middle of the fun.

"Mornin' fellas." Cooper's voice sounded friendly, but his face was blank. "We're wondering if you could help us."

The group looked at each other; some kept their eyes on the ground.

"Are you lost?" Jeb said.

"No. We're looking for somebody. Ezra Teague. Any of you fellas know him?"

Several shook their heads; most didn't react at all.

One of the young boys who had been dancing—a tall, gangly, funny looking boy—grinned and pointed off into the woods.

"I seen him about a month ago down there fishing, and he walked up and give me the trout he caught."

"Which way?" Cooper asked.

"Over there." The boy pointed, but then he turned in the opposite direction. "Or maybe it was that way." He grinned at this dancing buddy.

"Listen, you little—" Smith started, but Cooper put his hand on his chest.

Watching from the doorway, Blevins didn't like the direction things were taking. These were his customers. This was his property. There wasn't going to be any trouble here today. He picked up his old pistol from behind the counter.

The storekeeper stepped onto the porch, with one hand out of sight under his apron, and looked at the soldiers steadily.

"Pay no attention. He don't know nothing about it."

"Thank you for the help. Sorry to bother you." Cooper motioned with his hand, and Smith reluctantly followed. As soon as they were out of earshot, he demanded to know why they didn't persist.

"Because, dumbass. Didn't you notice a couple of hands moving inside their coats and overalls? These people don't take much to answering questions. We'll find him—don't worry. He's some lazy, dumb farmer wandering around missing his mama. We'll catch him."

But after a week in the area, it was time to report back to Camp Lee, which the detail was glad to do. They reported back to Nettles and urged him to send someone else to look for who they called 'those dumb crackers.'

Nettles knew that Teague and others like him were becoming more and more of a problem. The hangings in Georgia hadn't helped. The war was becoming unpopular; the sense of urgency, of nationalism and its interests, simply wasn't that strong.

Nettles really hadn't expected Cooper and Smith to be successful and really didn't want them to be. Careers are advanced by solving problems, and other than the war itself, these deserters were the Army's biggest problem right now. Nettles scheduled a meeting with some top brass and asked for permission to go to southwest Virginia.

"I'll enlist some local guides and locate some of the shiftless cowards myself," Nettles said.

"All right," the base commander said. "but remain very low-key about it. Stay out of the papers, or you'll only make things worse. And take Smith and Cooper back with you since they already know the area." Nettles saluted and left the room. He got up early the next morning, expecting that he would have everything in order, from the paperwork to packing and provisions, and would be on the train to Gate City that day.

But it was not to be. As usual, the military people were arguing with the political people in the War Department over what to do about the deserters and non-reporters. The little piece of paper clearing Nettles to go look for Ezra and the other missing men took several months to make its way back up and down the long chain of command.

Chapter 7

NETTLES AND HIS MEN HUNT EZRA

For the first time, Ezra became aware that the sheriff wasn't the only one looking for him. This was bad news. Sheriff Carter was a longtime family friend, plus it wasn't long until the next election. Ezra knew he wasn't going to look too hard for him. But an Army detail was something else. Why would the Army waste manpower like that when there's a war on, Ezra wondered?

The encounter with them had been almost funny. Ezra was walking back from the creek late one evening about sunset when he noticed some tracks in the soft clay. He froze and listened and sniffed the air. In the distance, he heard a low rumble of voices. He moved back down along the creek bank, walked down below them, and then climbed a steep bank above his campsite. *My plan worked, camping here in this bowl shaped clearing.* As he crawled on his belly and elbows to the crest, he could hear their voices plainly. They were only 20 feet or so away. Ezra's heart was pumping so loudly in his ears, he was afraid they could hear it, too.

"Looky here! He writes in a book like a girl!" A tall, gaunt young man with a boyish face was rifling the pages of his journal with black fingers. He and the other man laughed then as they moved to begin rummaging through the contents of the little knapsack behind the rocks that held his Bible, some shells, a big knife for skinning, and a skillet. Ezra knew he would have to act or they would take them. He crept down closer to them on his hands and knees. He slowly pulled out Father and Son and in one smooth motion, stood up, cocked them, and took a few steps down the hill. Only his head and shoulders were above the thicket, and he held both pistols straight out at eye level toward the men.

"You boys wasn't raised right." He leveled one of the guns at the tall one. "You forgot to knock."

The short one kept his hands in the air, but he tried to grin at Ezra.

"You ain't as big as they said you was."

"I want you to turn and go out of here. You boys ain't got a bit of manners."

The tall one was looking a little more nervous now. "You're crazy, mister."

Ezra raised the other pistol and pointed it at them so that both men were looking down a barrel. "I'm gonna give you a running start out of here, then I'm sending Father and Son to come after you." Ezra motioned with first one, then the other gun.

The two men looked at each other for the first time for just a second, then they turned and bolted through the brush, running and flailing their arms. Ezra could hear them breaking through the woods for quite a while. As soon as all grew silent again, he grabbed his things and took off in the opposite direction, dropping off into the creek, running through the water, scattering mud and minnows as he went. He ran and ran until he could run not more. He crawled into a laurel thicket, used his knapsack as a pillow, and slept away the afternoon.

When Ezra woke up, it was just beginning to lighten up. He crawled out of the thicket, his stomach rumbling. *I can't afford to hunt anything this morning. Those fellows could still be around here.* He looked up at the steep cliff in front of him and sighed. *If I want to eat,* he thought, and began picking his way up the steep rocks. On the other side, the land was cleared and the walking easy, which was good thing since his legs felt wobbly and weak from hunger and from the exertion of scaling the cliff.

He watched from the woods at the edge of the clearing and saw the Holzer girls out hanging the day's wash already. *Good girls. Some fellows will be lucky to get them.* Ezra blushed as he remembered the first time they fed him. He was sitting out on a rock in the creek after a bath, letting the sun warm and dry his skin. He was far, far from any houses or farms and thought it was safe to rest for a while. Standing on the warm rock, the air was blowing across his skin and the sun warmed him and stopped the shivers from the icy mountain water. He felt so glad to be alive and energized that he began to sing one of the crazy songs he learned down at the last barn dance.

"A preacher went out huntin,' t'was on one Sunday morn
Against his religion he took his gun along.
He shot himself three mighty fine quail
And one little measly hare.
And on his way returning home
Saw a great big grizzly bear.

Now the bear marched out in the middle o' the road
And waltzed to the preacher, you see
Preacher go so excited he climbed up a 'simmon tree.
The bear sat down on the ground.

The preacher climbed out on a limb.
He cast his eyes to the Lord in the skies
And these words he said to him:

Oh, Lordy, didn't you deliver Daniel from the lion's den?
And Jonah from the belly of a whale, and then
Three Hebrew children from the fiery furnace?
So the Good Book do declare.
Now, oh Lord, if you can't help me,
Well, then, please don't' cha help that bear!"

At that moment, a burst of giggles came from the direction of some brush. *Oh my Lord, do deliver me! I've stood here like a fool, naked and singing out loud, and now I'm caught for sure,* Ezra thought, grabbing his clothes, trying to cover himself and run at the same time. His eyes wild with panic, he whirled first one way and then another, realizing there was nowhere to go but in the direction of the sound. The little Holzer girl and her older sister had stepped out into the clearing then, and Ezra turned away and hurriedly put on his pants.

"You're him, aren't you?" the oldest one said. "We're sorry; we won't tell anybody."

Next thing he knew, he was sitting in their little kitchen drinking good coffee and eating fresh ham like a starved hound. Ezra chuckled to himself, remembering the questions from the little one.

"How many have you had to kill? Is it true you eat animals raw? You gotta wife?" Her father made her hush up and leave him alone. The older daughter stared at him, too, but he made himself not stare back, even though she was pretty.

But this time, Ezra knew he couldn't risk going to their cabin. He crept down through the woods until he was near enough to signal them. He cupped his hands to his mouth and gave a few bird calls, then gobbled like a turkey. The little one tugged on her sister's skirt, and they both looked in his direction. He stepped out from behind a tree and motioned for them to come to him. The littlest called her dog, and they came running toward him.

"It's you. What's the matter?" She kept her distance from Ezra, kneeling down to hold the dog.

"I hate to bother you all again, but I'm really, really hungry. Do you have anything you could bring me?"

"Come on in, and Mama will fix you some eggs."

"No, I can't. I need you to bring it without telling your Mama."

The little girl ran back to the clothesline then and talked to her sister. The girl had now hung clothes and quilts on both lines, and she was standing between them looking in Ezra's direction. She held up her palm to Ezra, then put the other palm, too, signaling "Wait." Then the girls disappeared into the house. Ezra waited and waited. His stomach was really hurting now. *They're not coming back. They're afraid now.* But in a few minutes, the back door swung open, and here came the little one back carrying a bucket.

Ezra saw her mother appear at the door, and he shrank back. The little one stopped at the edge of the garden and poured some of the contents of the bucket out. The mother stepped away from the door then. The little one immediately stopped pouring and broke into a trot toward him.

"I'm sorry. This is the best I can do." She looked back over her shoulder at the door and dumped the contents of the bucket on the ground. She turned then and ran back to the house.

There in front of him on the ground was a soggy pile of biscuits soaked in grease and a little gravy, some bits of scrambled eggs, and a slab of bacon. *I better get busy or the smell of this will draw dogs and God knows what else.* Ezra picked up the chunks out of the grass and wolfed them down. He felt ashamed. *What would Eva say? Eating nastiness out of somebody's slop bucket.* Tears burned as the corners of his eyes, but he did not let them fall.

EZRA'S JOURNAL

Bible Time

I just went back and read what I been writing in my journal, and I realized I forgot something. I said in my very first page that I was going to write down my prayers, and I haven't done that. I guess because I was so tired and scared and nervous at first that all my prayers were just short "God please help me" prayers. I'm getting more used to living like this now, and I don't know why, but I don't feel as scared as I did. I'm sleeping a little better. I've been going over to the cave to take naps.

I also think that I am not as afraid as I was because I've been just sitting quiet for a good part of the day and reading my Bible. I've always read it now and then when I get time, but my real studying was only done in church or Bible School in the summer. I never really just studied over it like I have lately. I read a passage and think about it a little, then I read it again. I've started to see that reading scripture and really understanding it is two different things. I remember hearing preachers say that before, but I didn't really think about it. I think writing about it in this book will be the best thing I could do.

I remember a traveling evangelist one time talked about his wife keeping a prayer journal. She wrote down who and what needed praying for, and she would write down the prayers. Sometimes, he said, she would send the prayers to the people she was praying for. I can't do that right now, but I could write them down and give them to them later. That would be a good idea. James 5:16 says

"The effectual fervent prayer of a righteous man availeth much."
So here goes.

Dear Lord: first, always, I want to thank you for another day.
Thank you for that rabbit you sent, and for the sack of sweet
potatoes the Smiths left for me in their back pasture. I ask today
that you would bless Eva and help her during this trying time. If
you could just touch her on the shoulder, Lord, and tell her I'm
all right, I'm well and finding something to eat. Nobody deserves
a good day more than Eva, Lord. Forgive me for thinking about
just giving up and killing myself. Forgive me where I've failed you,
and help me to know what's the right thing to do. Please give me
strength to just keep on like I am and wait upon the Lord. Amen.

A Scare

I just had a close call. It was just getting daylight, and I was
walking toward the river just below Fort Blackmore. I was gonna
go down there and see if there might be a party of hunters down
there that I could get a biscuit off of. I'm really starting to miss
biscuits, I dream about them some nights. Anyway, as I started
off the hill toward the bridge, I seen a man standing there in a
uniform with a gun on his hip. It like to scared me to death. It
wasn't a sheriff's uniform, it was an Army uniform. The Army has
posted guards down here on the bridges. I can't believe they'd
want me that bad, to waste men down here standing around on
bridges when there's a war on.

Hoping for Spring 1919

I've been reading in Colossians in the New Testament and it says in chapter 3, "Now put off all these; anger, wrath, malice blasphemy, filthy communication out of your mouth." Those first four are fairly easy. When you get mad, you should bite your tongue, because what's going to come out will not be good. And, of course, the gossip about your neighbors is not good. Blasphemy is cursing God, so that's just common sense that you don't need to be doing that.

But that last part about filthy communication is harder. I believe that's talking about cussing and dirty jokes. When I ask forgiveness, I believe that most of what needs forgiving concerns these two. I cannot stop myself from cussing. It's like a sneeze or a laugh, especially under tight circumstances. James must have been talking about me when he wrote, "But the tongue can no man tame, it is an unruly evil, full of deadly poison."

Momma washed my mouth out with soap a lot when I was little, but then she finally just gave up because I got so big. If I stumped my toe or hit my finger with a hammer, I'd say a bad word. What used to make Momma madder than that though was that I thought cussing was funny.

The Mooney family that lived over the hill from us wasn't church people, and every other word out of any of them's mouth was usually a cuss word. We used to give that littlest boy of theirs a nickel to cuss for us. We called him a cussing machine. We'd give him the money, and he'd start. He was just a little fellow, maybe 4 or 5, and he couldn't talk real plain. We'd hand him the nickel, and he'd start—Dat damn dog a daddy's, he da cwaziest sumbitch you ever saw—and on and on. Till one day Momma caught us doing it and like to beat my legs off with a switch from her yellowbush in the backyard. She said we was tempting that child just like the Devil himself, and she better never catch me doing such as that again. I minded her, but that still doesn't mean my heart's right. I still think it was funny.

<u>Two Days Later</u>

I found out about the man on the bridge. I found an old newspaper out in the trash behind the Blevins' store. It said the Army had asked the new VA militia company to post guards at all the bridges in case any of them German spies was to try to come around. That scares me to death to hear it. I don't know what a German looks like and wouldn't recognize one of them if I saw him. I feel bad that I'm not doing anything to help stop them if they're coming in over here and spying on us in America.

I read about a lot of other stuff that was happening in that paper. It was good to know a little bit about the world in one way, and bad in another. It said that the War Department in Washington was asking women to try to not waste food because it would help win the war. Most women, unless they are no count, would never waste food anyway, whether the government tells them to or not. Eva, she has it figured out just about exactly how much beans or potatoes or cornbread it takes to feed us, and she makes just enough. You have to be rich to be wasting food.

The worst thing I read about in the paper is this bad sickness has really hit here, a epidemic the paper called it. I had hoped it was just in the Army, but it's here now, pretty bad. I had already heard a little about it in Eva's last note. She said that many people were sick, more than she could ever remember, and two people who were some kin to us had died. They was distant kin, cousins on the McConnell side, but I was sad anyway 'cause I remember their momma from family reunions.

Grouse Hunting

I flushed three grouse today, and it took probably five years off my life. They always scare you to death when they come up. There is no question that grouse hunting is the best thing in the world, bar none. Well, since there's some important things I haven't experienced yet, I better not say that for sure. But I can be positive that it's either the best or next to best. I would never have known about grouse hunting if it weren't for Judge Hilton. Now, anybody can go grouse hunting if they have a shotgun, and I'd kicked some up before when I was out deer hunting, but that ain't the same. A man's gotta have a dog to do it right.

Judge Hilton he had the most beautiful little bitch you ever saw, named Maggie. I had never seen this kind of dog. She was white with big black spots and a few liver ones. He said she was a certain kind of English Setter, and he had her sent all the way from England from a fellow name Louellan, I'm not sure how to spell it. She's kind of a long-haired dog with a long tail, and she beats anything you ever saw. When she smells a bird, she will freeze just like stone, and her front paw picks up off the ground and her nose sorta down and her tail straight back, pointed straight in the direction of where the bird is.

The Judge even let me shoot his fine shotgun. He is a good man and really liked me, I guess because I always help him with his hay and things. In one day hunting we saw 17 birds, and the Judge killed three of them and I killed one. A grouse flushes and flies awful fast, and if you ain't in real good practice, you won't hit them. But we had enough that Mrs. Hilton fixed them for us for supper, and it was the sweetest meat I ever tasted.

The Bible speaks had about not coveting what another man has, and I sure don't begrudge that dog to the Judge. But that would be something to own a dog such as that.

Visit to Momma

I went to visit Momma's grave today. I couldn't hardly stand it long. I pulled some weeds around the headstone and talked to her some. I'm not crazy yet, and I know she can't hear me. It felt good though, and nobody was around to think I was touched. I spent a good bit of time in there, in the cemetery, because I got interested in walking around looking at the tombstones and what they said. Eva put "A tender mother and a faithful woman" on Momma's headstone, and I got such an ache in my throat when I read it that I had to go sit under a shade tree and cry for a while. I got up finally and went and read some of the other tombstones before it got so dark I couldn't see. Several just had short ones like "Asleep in Jesus" or "Rest in peace" or "We will meet again." But there were two long ones that I copied down—

His toils are past, his work is done, he fought the fight, he kept the faith. And this one was my favorite——The soul has now taken its flight, to mansions of glory above to mingle with angels of light and dwell in the Kingdom of love. The soul taking flight——that is a beautiful thing to think about. I would see Momma's soul as one of her little bluebirds that she loved so much.

This gives me an idea of something to do besides just thinking about how tired or hungry I am. I'm gonna go around to some of the cemeteries and look at the headstones and copy down what they say. That'll be interesting.

Chapter 8

EVA MAKES MONEY

As the winter chill began to close in, the leaves long gone from the trees, Eva had faced the Christmas season with a heavy heart. There was ham in the smokehouse and plenty of food put up from past gardens. But with her mother out in the cemetery, her father lost in his silent world, Ezra gone, these absent voices were all she could think about. On the days when it rained all day or dark clouds hovered, the front room with only one little window would grow dark as her mood.

Eva always felt better with the front door open, with the light and the smells of hay and mint drifting in on the breeze, and from April to November, her first steps every morning were to open it, even before she made coffee or lit the cookstove. Every fall when it was time to shut the door for the winter, there would be a tightness in her chest and a heaviness in her legs, and at night her sleep was restless and fitful.

The dreams would always start in winter, too, and that was another reason for Eva to dread it. As she would sink into sleep, she would always see David's face floating by, laughing and sweating like he just came in from the field. She would see him ashen-faced and thin lying in bed as the diphtheria took him. It was strange how his death was all her dreams brought her, almost never happy images of his courting her, their lovemaking, working in the garden together. But at least it was some consolation that the baby she had lost always appeared in her dreams fat and blonde, sitting on her lap, the smooth roundness of her little legs and toes as clear and vivid as if she were alive. Eva would rise exhausted, have a little breakfast, and after chores, get out her quilt basket. The cloth and the stitching were her friends, and she talked to her quilts because there was no one else now.

But the quilts were more than companions and an outlet for her anxiety. They were the family's only income now. Eva had contracted with a group of ladies in Big Stone Gap who were selling them to churches up north. They paid her $10 a quilt for the baby quilts, and sometimes $20 or more for a big one—a small fortune! Eva hid the money in a jar under the floor and didn't let anyone see where it was. *I wish I could get Daddy to understand what I'm doing. He would be so tickled,* she thought.

Eva knew all of the common patterns: the Double Wedding Ring, the Flower Basket, the Log Cabin, the Trip Around the World. The first quilt she ever had was a Double Wedding Ring that her mother made for her when Eva was 14 and packed away for her wedding day. The first quilt Eva made herself was the Log Cabin she made that first long winter after she married while David worked at the sawmill.

As she waited for her baby that next winter, too sick to eat, her feet too swollen to walk, a Crazy Quilt was all she could muster. It wound up unfinished, uneven with jagged edges like the rest of her life, after their little girl was born early and sick. When they buried her under the shade of the poplar grove, she was wrapped in that quilt.

David had tiptoed around her that spring, said little, but watched her always with those piercing black eyes of his, blaming her somehow, Eva thought. To fight the swirling sick thoughts in her head, Eva quilted right on through the summer that year, even as the weather grew sticky hot. She made a Drunkard's Path, a blinding blue and pink kaleidoscope of color and shape like the one she saw at the Wise County fair. The spinning wheel, the butter churn, her flower and vegetable garden were all left untouched that year, as the house grew silent, more dusty, more stale every day. Eva would quilt for days without end, stopping only to cook and eat a little. Her hair would string down, and her clothes would stain and smell from perspiration, but she wouldn't take time to wash but every other day or so.

When the first chill of winter came in the air that fall, Eva shut the door and went to bed. For the first few days, she sat in bed and quilted some when she was awake. She quit talking, quit cooking, quit cleaning. David stayed with her, so he lost his sawmill job. By November, the store wouldn't give them more credit, and they had eaten the last of the food. With no credit, there was no flour or cornmeal to make bread, and David paced the house with a gaunt, hunted look.

"Get up. Get up, Eva." He finally began begging her. "I have to go to work."

She ignored him at first. But then one afternoon when she woke up from another nap, she found him sitting in the floor with her quilt pieces spread out between his legs like a child, holding the needle and thread in that awkward way only a man can.

"I'm going crazy, too." He looked at her then, and it was as if Eva just recognized who he was. "I've got to do something to get us some money." She sat up and threw back the covers and got down in the floor with him. She took the scissors and thread from his hand. "Go get me some firewood," she said. "I can't quilt when my hands are so cold."

In a week's time, using every scrap of cloth she had, including tearing up some old aprons, one of her dad's rotten workshirts, and even a small piece of cloth she had been saving for the baby, Eva created her own wild pattern and called it "Robbing Peter to Pay Paul." She sold it to Mrs. Slemp, the rich lady from Big Stone Gap, and took the money straight to the store.

Now her quilts were helping her keep everything going for a second time. Not only was she earning a little money from them, but taking them to town for Mrs. Slemp to have picked up gave her cover for taking things to Ezra. She would roll notes, ammunition, pencils, and little drawings into the quilts and drop them off at the springs or the cave, or one of the other couple of places Ezra felt were safe enough. Even if someone were watching the house or watching her in town, she just looked to be a woman in a wagon with a quilt or two in the back. The few times she had taken something bulky to drop off, she had known better than to risk laying those in the back with the quilts where someone might notice the lumps. She had carried an iron skillet once, and another time, Ezra's big skinning knife, between her legs as she walked out of the house. She grinned at the thought of it. *If anybody was watching me, they must've thought I was awful constipated or something.*

It was on one of these trips to deliver quilts to town and a note to Ezra that she got the good news she'd been waiting for. As she rode into town that day, she noticed people standing around in big groups everywhere, smiling and nodding, and children running everywhere. Everyone seemed happy. *What in the world is going on?* As she got off the wagon and started into Christian's Department Store she caught sight of a newspaper pinned up behind the counter. "ARMISTICE SIGNED—The War's Over!" The headline read. Eva grabbed up the paper, her mouth open, and looked around at the storekeepers.

"I guess you hadn't heard." Mrs. Christian said. "It's finally over."

"Thank God!" Eva wanted to cry, but she couldn't let herself start, not here. *It's over; he's safe. They won't come after him now.*

After she chatted a few minutes and tried to act as normal as she could, Eva raced outside and sat down under a shade tree near the courthouse steps. She took out the note she had tucked in her pocket and wrote the good news on the back.

Ezra:
You won't believe what has happened. The war is over. You are out of trouble. All the troops will be coming home soon and you can come, too. My prayers have been answered, and I will thank God and praise him today and forever for this lifting of our burdens. Your loving sister, Eva

With the money from the quilts she had delivered, full of relief and happiness that Ezra would soon be home, Eva allowed herself a little treat: she bought a piece of cheese and some crackers at the store and ate them under a tree. People stared at her as they went by, but she didn't care. *I deserve a picnic*, she grinned to herself. When she finished, she set off for the spring to deliver her good-news note.

Chapter 9

ALMA THINKS
IT'S OVER

When word came that the war was over, Alma was beside
herself with joy and relief. She went into a cleaning and
cooking frenzy, baking pies and sweet potatoes, and washing
and ironing the curtains. She sent her father to gather up all
the relatives and friends he could, and they all gathered around
the long table, happy together in a way that they hadn't seen in
a long, long time. Alma was almost giddy, laughing and cutting
up with her cousins, even singing a little song for them at the
piano, something Sam Newton had never been able to persuade
her to do before, and he was a bit puzzled at her gregariousness.

Little did he know that Alma's excitement wasn't the typical
relief being felt by the rest of the family, but was connected to
her big secret—she was in love with Ezra Teague and was going

to marry him. For some reason Alma didn't quite understand herself, his predicament had only made him more attractive to her. She didn't know if it was the daring, rebellious nature of it that excited her, or the unbelievable nobility of his willingness to make such a sacrifice for his mother that had sealed her heart to him. But whatever the reason, she had made up her mind about it, and there would be no changing it. With the war over, Ezra would come home again, one way or the other, and she was going to see to it that he realized that she was his 'home' now.

After the couple of days of celebrating with her family, Alma rode over to Eva's and took her one of the apple pies that were left over. Eva greeted her at the door with the first real smile Alma had seen from her, and she took the pie straight to the kitchen table and cut a big slice. They talked and giggled like schoolgirls.

"Have you heard from Ezra?"

"No," Eva said, and sipped her coffee. She leaned closer to Alma and lowered her voice. Sheriff Carter came here the other day. He said Ezra still wasn't in the clear. Said they still needed soldiers, and they wasn't going to just forget about Ezra. I'm talking low so Daddy won't hear. Sometimes if I say Ezra's name, he looks at me like he's hisself, and I'm afraid he might be understanding something about what's going on."

Alma felt like she'd been kicked by Diamond.

"But why? With the war over, surely they don't need so many. You all need Ezra worse than the Army."

Alma's raised voice roused the old man, and he whimpered and jabbered like a baby. Eva put her finders to her lips and frowned. She grasped Alma by the shoulders.

"Keep your voice down! No point in upsetting him." Alma looked over at the old man asleep in the chair, his mouth open wide, his face gaunt and collapsing in on itself.

"Ezra has to turn himself in. That's what the man said. If he does, they'll go easy on him. He's got to come in and be punished. He said the Army's dead set on it. I don't know if he knows what he's talking about or not."

She reached over and patted Alma's hand and rubbed it. "Don't worry. When Ezra gets home, everything will be all right."

Chapter 10

NETTLES COMES TO TOWN

As the train pulled into the station, Nettles felt the sense of unease he always felt when he was down in his home part of the state. The hills were so tall all around in every direction, it seemed, so that he felt he was down in a deep feather-ticked mattress like his Grandmother Nettles had. He felt anxious, smothered. He liked the flat land better.

When he got his luggage, he set out toward the only hotel in town. The old Boatright Hotel had just opened under new owners and was now The Compton Hotel. It was certainly not as grand as some hotels in the area such as The Martha Washington Inn in Abingdon, but it was clean and pleasant, and the food was good. Nettles had stayed there once before when he had come down to meet with some local officials on recruiting issues.

In the dining room, Nettles ordered fried chicken. A stranger in a military uniform drew a few stares from the staff and patrons, but Nettles just nodded in recognition and said nothing. His little waitress, a waif of a girl so small she looked like a child, told him her name was Julieanna and tried to make small talk.

"I s'pose you're here about the militias." She kept his coffee cup filled to the brim, partly to have an excuse to come back and attempt to pry some information, Nettles thought, and partly because there were only two other customers besides him, leaving her with little to do. Nettles looked at her levelly and decided two could play this little game of questions.

"Actually I'm here to look up an old friend, Ezra Teague. Do you know him?"

Her face didn't change except for the eyes. "Never heard of him. Sorry." She moved off into the kitchen with her coffee pot and didn't come back until his meal was ready. She sat it in front of him and disappeared without another word.

Nettles enjoyed his meal. The chicken was so crisp on the outside but really tender and moist on the inside, just like his grandmother used to make. When he finished, he sat on the front porch of the inn and watched the various pedestrians and horses and buggies go by. There was an occasional automobile, but with the heavy ruts and mud holes at various places down the main street and the rest of the county roads little more than paths, they were the exception. He would need a good horse, that's for sure.

The next morning he set out at daybreak toward Fort Blackmore first. As he crossed the ridge above the Clinch River, he stopped and stared for a long time. A steep wall of rock stood to the right of him, and the river was a marshy sand bar to the left, along the railroad line. In his notebook, he made meticulous notes about the landmarks, both natural and manmade, about the topography of the land, and about the watersheds. He would stop off in country stores and along fields where people were working to ask the names of creeks and information about which direction they flowed and into which river, the Holston or the Clinch. Over the next several days, he rode and camped all over the county. He explored the Big Moccasin Creek watershed up to Nicklesville, across the old wagon road at Hamilton Gap into the Hiltons community, and finally, the whole Copper Creek area from Gate City to Fort Blackmore. Exhausted, he came back to the Compton Hotel to take a bath and sleep and think.

After the hot bath, meal, and long, deep sleep, Nettles returned to the row of rockers on the front porch and studied over his notes. He felt fairly familiar with the terrain in general terms now, but he knew he had no chance against a native like Teague who knew every inch of the area and loved the outdoors.

Like his native Wise County, Scott County was rugged, spectacular place. As he rode along, he would come through dense woods with steep hills or walls of rock on both sides, only to suddenly emerge into an opening into the air. The views in some places literally took his breath away. Nettles would be astonished to realize how high up in the air he was because the climb was so gradual and the forest so thick.

The county recorder's office had given him some maps and documents that the railroad company had printed up. Nettles was surprised that much of Scott County was in the 2000 feet elevation range. Part of one of the narrowest parts of the Great Valley of Virginia, it's as if Mother Nature squeezed the edges of the valley together, pushing the mountains, hills, valleys and rivers ever closer. The major geographical feature is Clinch Mountain, which extends around thirty miles, winding like a snake across much of the county. At its highest point, it's over 3100 feet above sea level. Its little sister, Moccasin Ridge, runs almost parallel and is over 2300 feet at its highest point. There were two rivers, the Holston and the Clinch, and three major creeks in the county that were difficult to cross: Copper Creek, Big Moccasin Creek, and Possum Creek. There were caves and steep cliffs of rock in many places.

Nettles knew Teague would stay mainly in the areas of Clinch Mountain between Gate City and Fort Blackmore and in the southern end of Copper Ridge because that would be the area he was most familiar with, and he could walk in a day or two to his home place. That knowledge was little consolation, however. There was quite a bit of cleared land in both those areas, but that didn't help all that much in terrain like this. Scott County's farmers mainly were animal herders of cows, sheep, chickens, and pigs. The land that was fenced was pasture, still very overgrown with trees and brush and tall weeds that cows wouldn't eat, not nice big flat fields of corn or wheat or hay like in the rest of the state. Nettles had marveled as he traveled around at the cattle standing and grazing on land that was steep as his horse's face. The locals joked that they had to breed special cows with two legs on one side shorter than the other so they could stand up.

A man who was as familiar with the area, resourceful, and hardy as Teague would be extremely difficult to find here. And Nettles had gotten the strong sense during his little excursion that the locals were not going to be inclined to help in the search at all. There were several from the county besides Teague that were in hiding, and the sheriff didn't seem too anxious to put effort into bringing them in. The locals had been willing enough to give directions and information about geography when he asked, but both times he'd made the mistake of mentioning Teague's name, people had clamped their jaws shut tighter than bear traps and excused themselves from the conversation at first opportunity. Nettles had decided on a less direct approach, and he had his little waitress friend to thank for the idea.

At supper that evening when she came to take his order, he tried to smile and exchange pleasantries, but it was an unnatural exercise for him.

"By the way, you mentioned the local militia forming the other day. How might I go about attending one of their meetings? I would be happy to offer my considerable expertise to assist in this important effort."

"Just a minute," she said and scurried away.

Oh no, another one I've scared off, he thought. Just then a fat man wiping his hands in his apron came out of the kitchen toward him.

"I'm John Carter, sir. I understand you was wanting information about the local militia efforts. I'm in the group that was beginning to get things organized, but we reckoned there was no need now that the war was over. What can I do for you?"

"No sir. Wars don't end like a schoolyard game. It'll take another year or two to get things squared away." Nettles wiped his mouth again. "I would appreciate the opportunity to talk to your group. I'm here in the area helping some other communities with getting the program started, and I thought I could perhaps be of assistance."

Carter shrugged, said something about that being up to Nettles, and walked away. He came back with a meeting notice he had prepared for the local newspaper and pointed the way to their office.

"I'll take care of this. Hope to see you at the meeting. Thank you, Mr. Carter, and God bless America."

Nettles knew that, barring death or natural calamity, he would be at the meeting for sure because the militia group would be the key to helping him find Ezra.

When Nettles got to the meeting place, he was disappointed but not surprised that there were only about half a dozen men there in front of the school. These folks weren't educated, but they weren't stupid, either. The government had called up all of the country's National Guards and urged the formation of new militias. The men knew that the forming of the local citizen militias could eventually land them at the front lines. Nettles made sure to wipe the disappointment off his face and replace it with a pleasant smile as he stepped forward to introduce himself to the group.

Nettles noticed one of the men immediately. Although the man was of medium build, he looked to be in excellent shape, with broad shoulders, big arms, and a darkly tanned face that looked to be outdoors a great deal. Nettles introduced himself to the group and made small talk with them about the war, the military, and the weather. They were much more interested in the last topic, and their conversation grew more lively as they talked about their crops and their plans for work the coming week.

They really aren't interested in the war, Nettles thought. *These dumb farmers don't care about anything outside their little world.*

A couple of more men showed up, maybe sixteen years old, Nettles thought, with long, skinny faces and dirty hands, and they started the meeting. They seemed to expect Nettles to lead the meeting, so he did, giving them an update on developments on the front and explaining why local groups like this were being formed to guard bridges and railroads.

"We need to be alert, gentlemen, to German spies and to their sympathizers in this country who might aid their cause." Nettles wasn't sure how realistic this concern was, but many in Washington continued to push the idea as a way to garner support and get the local militias to organize.

The men listened, some with their mouths hung open, staring vacantly. Only the stout one Nettles had been watching, who introduced himself as Mac, spoke up.

"Lieutenant Nettles, what exactly does a German look like? I wouldn't know one if I see one. Are they dark-skinned people?"

"No," Nettles said. "That's the thing. They look just like you people, fair-skinned and light hair mostly. They could move among you easily, and that's why we think they might choose this area to penetrate and blow up the railroad system."

The men stirred then and looked at each other.

"We'll talk to some more folks, and take it from there," Mac said and stood up. The others rose then, shook hands with each other, and several came up and shook Nettles' hand. Then they left. Nettles wasn't really sure what had just happened.

Nettles hurried outside and called to Mac. "I'd like to talk to you a minute about something. I need your help."

Mac sat down on the school house steps and listened intently, his eyes never leaving Nettles' face the entire time, while the lieutenant told about Teague and two other men from Duffield who were AWOL from Camp Lee. He railed about the irresponsibility of it, about the lack of patriotism, about the soldiers from Scott County who were over on the front, dying in trenches and breathing mustard gas, until he wore himself out.

"Will you help me?"

Mac's face was expressionless. He looked at the ground for a long moment, and then stood up. "I'll show you around the area. I know the county pretty good. I'll teach you about tracking, so you can catch these people. But I won't be a part of taking any of them in. I have to live here."

The next day, daylight found the two men riding out of Gate City with provisions for several days, out along Copper Creek bluff and through some of the most beautiful, most intimidating geography Nettles had ever seen. Mac didn't say much as they rode along, but he would stop periodically and point out breaks in the ridges, old trails and log roads, and some old dilapidated buildings almost buried in weeds and vines that could be possible shelter.

"What about caves?" Nettles asked. "I've heard that some of these men have been found hiding in caves."

"They's a few around here," Mac said, "but most of them aren't big enough for a man to try to live in. He might crawl in there and sleep in one of them."

"If you were him," Nettles paused for a minute, hoping the question wouldn't offend, "where would you hide?"

"I wouldn't." A hint of a grin tugged at the corner of Mac's mouth. "I'd do just what he's doing. Keep moving."

EZRA'S JOURNAL

Winter 1919

Sweet Eva brought me more ammunition, a pencil, some cornbread still warm and buttery—God bless her—and my uniform all pressed and laying flat on a quilt covered with another quilt. The biggest news is that the war is over. I can't hardly believe. If I had stayed in, I would have probably just got there. That would have made me mad as the devil, to go to all that trouble, training for months and then the long ride over there, just to have to turn around and come back.

I hoped she was going to tell me that this was all over, that I could just come on in now that they ain't no war to fight. But she says Sheriff Carter says otherwise. Says that the Army has done said that there will be lots of troops needed over there for maybe a year or two and them that has run off are still in big trouble. The feelings I have are hard to put into words. I know why she brought the uniform. The sheriff has told her that things will go easier on me if I'm in uniform; she told me in her last letter. After all this, the war is over. Things will start to get back like they was before now, except I still don't see any way out of this for me.

I feel so bad for putting Eva through all this worry. I've always felt closer to her than to some of the other ones, though I love them all, I guess because she was like a momma to me. I can remember even as a little shaver looking up at her, my big sister, who seemed so big then, holding my hand and taking me down to the creek, showing me crawdads and little mussels. I see her then, I see her now, and I just can't write no more right now, Book. I can't see for the tears.

Wanted Man

Walking toward the store to find a newspaper, I see a piece of paper stuck up on a tree and when I got closer, I couldn't believe my eyes. It said "Ezra Teague——Wanted by U. S. Army." It listed some other names, too, but I didn't know any of them. I just stood and stared and stared. I would never have thought such a thing. To see your name up on a poster like a criminal is a real bad feeling. I started to just walk on like somebody stupid, but then I had sense enough to walk back and tear it down.

It had a description of all three of us. It said I was 180 pounds. I laughed about that since I've got so skinny out here my bones are poking out like an old milk cow. And it said I was last seen near the Wise County line. That's funny, too, because whoever seen me in Wise County is either drinking too much or seeing ghosts.

Rumors of War

I found an old newspaper that says that German spies may be all around. I don't know if it's still true or not, now that the war's over, but it made a chill a run down my back. A lot of the rumors about it have turned out to be false, though. One story said that Germans were going around to the houses of black folks and poor whites and saying they were from the government and they were there to inventory their food. Then later, some of these folks were being robbed, or these people who claimed to be from the government would say they need to take some of their food, by order of the President, to send to our troops overseas, and some folks would just hand it over to them. Now you know that ain't German spies. That's just some common thieves taking advantage of circumstances! And I heard somebody come running up the front of Starnes Grocery that other day hollering "The Kaiser's been shot! The Kaiser's been shot!" but Joe Johnson was setting on the front porch whittling, and I heard him saying something about that not being true, the paper said so. It's just wild tale after wild tale.

Chapter 11

NETTLES VISITS EVA

When Nettles set out over the hills to the Teague's little mountain farm, he gave his men the afternoon off to go fishing. He knew Teague's sister was not going to be anything like cooperative anyway, but if he and his whole party came stampeding into her yard, she probably wouldn't even open the door. She might even shoot them!

As he came near the little house, he looked at the junk scattered across the porch and yard, the weeds growing up over the stone step up into the side door. There was firewood scattered all about in the back of the house, and Nettles could see a small ax buried in a big block of oak. He called out, "Hello!" and took his time getting off his horse. He hitched it slowly to the big fence post but made no move to open the gate. After a long moment, the front door opened a crack and what appeared to be a little girl pushed her face barely out. "Hello" he said again. "I'm Lieutenant Nettles from Camp Lee. I would like to talk to you for a few minutes about your brother, please."

"You can come in the gate" she said, and Nettles was startled by her voice. Her voice sounded older than he expected, tired but strong, and a little bit hoarse, like she wasn't used to talking. He thanked her and stepped through into the yard, taking off his hat as he went. He stopped and looked at her before he set his foot up on the first step up to the porch. She stepped out the door then and shut it behind her. "You can have a seat here if you want," and she pointed to an old bench against the wall. "But you're wasting your time. I don't know where Ezra is and I wouldn't tell you if I did." She crossed her arms and pursed her lips.

Nettles looked down at his hands. He thought he knew what he was going to say. He had a speech about patriotism and about duty and about the stupidity of Ezra's actions in all this, but something about the whole scene before him stopped him. The slightly sagging porch floor, the weeds and clutter, the soft wisp of hair falling down over the girl's eye, her thin hands, red and chapped. Nettles suddenly felt confused and tired.

"I hear you're a fine quilter," he said.

Eva looked startled. "Well, yes, I guess. How'd you know that?"

"I've seen you bringing your quilts to town." Eva's arms folded back in their defensive posture with this admission that Nettles had been spying on her. "I figure that's how you're getting notes or maybe even supplies to him. That's pretty smart. Who thought of that? You or him?"

"Why did you come here?" Eva demanded.

"I wanted to meet you, and I wanted you to meet me. It's nothing personal from me, you understand. I've got to do my duty."

"And Ezra had to do his!" She raised her voice a little, and her face flushed a little pink. At that moment there was a muffled cry and a thump from inside the house, and Eva whirled in an instant through the front door. Nettles followed, stepped just inside the door and stopped. Eva was trying to get her father, who had fallen out on the rough plank floor, back up in his chair by the window. Nettles rushed over and told her to stand aside. He picked the old man up in his arms and set him back upright.

"Daddy, Daddy, are you all right?" The old man didn't answer, but he looked blankly at Eva for a minute; then he just rested his hand back on his cheek and gazed out the window.

"He doesn't seem to be hurt." Nettles said. "How long has he been like this?"

"Almost two years." Eva answered. At that moment she realized how close they were, knelt down together at her father's chair, their bodies almost touching. Nettles had the same thought at the same moment and they rose simultaneously and took a little step back.

"I've really come here just to ask you to talk to your brother. It's time he came in. He could get hurt or killed out there. And he's sure not helping you any." Nettles looked at the old man again.

"So it's better for him to just come in and get hung, right? So you can get back to shining your boots, I reckon." Eva's voice grew a little louder again, but she caught herself and looked at her father. She stepped toward the door and motioned for Nettles to come back out on the porch.

"No, he won't be hung. That's what I wanted you to know. If Ezra comes in voluntarily, he gets leniency. If he keeps on, me or the sheriff or somebody will get him, and the Army's not going to be too happy with him."

Nettles was pleased to see a little change come over her face; he could sense her turning that over in her mind and how hopeful she was that it was true.

"Here," he said, and reached into his back pocket. "Here's a news article about it that came out a few days ago. Read it for yourself."

Eva took the paper out of his hand and walked over to the rocker by the window and sat down. He noticed as she tried to wipe the little tendril of hair out of her eyes in order to read that her hand was visibly trembling. Nettles studied her tense face. She was very pale and thin, and Nettles watched her try to suppress a cough as she studied the paper intently. He noticed then how really tiny she was, especially her little feet in those broken down old shoes, and his heart sank for her, for himself, for the situation everyone was in.

When she finished reading it, she stood up, handed it back to him, and stepped back away from him quickly.

"I heard about the war being over. Ezra won't get in any big trouble anyway, right? Why would the Army still look for him if there's no war going on?

Nettles knew he had to choose his words carefully. "You are right that the war is over and there won't be the need for so much manpower eventually. But for right now, there's still a great need and will be for at least a year until everything is finally returned to normal and all the troops rotate home. Ezra is still in trouble, Miss Teague. But he'll get a fair opportunity to tell his side of things, I assure you."

Eva felt tears welling up, her stomach tightening into knot. *Sheriff was right. He's not home free.*

"You need to go now. I've got to tend to him." She nodded toward her father and opened the front door.

"Will you at least tell your brother about my visit?" Nettles asked.

"I don't know. I'll think about it."

"I appreciate that. Is there anything I can do for you while I'm here? I notice you don't have much kindling in here. I'd be happy—"

"No thank you," Eva said levelly and stuck her chin out defiantly.

76

Nettles knew the matter was closed, so he thanked her again, put his hat on, and left quickly. Eva watched Nettles until he was out of sight and then hurriedly penned another note to Ezra, telling him that her earlier warning had been correct. He needed to know the Army was still serious about punishing him. She settled her father into his bed and wrapped him tightly in quilts. Then she put on her disguise and set off for the spring.

When Nettles got back to the campsite by the river, Mac was there, and Nettles told him what he'd done.

"She's a tough little nut," Nettles said, "but I think I may have made an impression on her."

Mac kind of chuckled then, and Nettles faces reddened a little. "What's so funny?"

"Eva Teague generally ain't easily impressed, and I doubt you changed that." Mac kind of grinned at him and chuckled again, and even Nettles had to smile a little. "She's kinda pretty, ain't she?"

Nettles didn't say anything, but Mac was pleased to see by his expression that he'd struck a little close to home with that one. "Hmphh," was all Nettles said, and he walked away from the campsite out through the woods, saying to Mac over his shoulder, "I'm going to take a nap. Wake me up when those yahoos get back from fishing."

Chapter 12

ALMA BIDES HER TIME

When Alma found out that Ezra's situation wasn't going to end immediately and that the end of the war did not mean the end of the Army's problem with Ezra and the other deserters, she sank into a brief depression. She moped around the house with her hair tied up in a scarf and snapped at her father when he asked about supper. As she had done so many times in the past, she turned to Diamond, the woods, and her childhood pastimes to get her through it. Although she knew it would upset her father to see her return to what he called her 'tomboy tomfoolery,' she returned to a habit she had only abandoned a few years earlier: she put on pants, a flannel shirt, suspenders, boots, and hat and tore off across the field at full gallop with the feel of her father's scowl burning into her back.

She beat her heels into Diamond's sides. The animal, sensing her anger and tenseness, bore down and dug deeper into the dirt, shooting it out in little sprays behind his hooves. They ran and ran until they both were exhausted, and Alma felt some release and slowed him to a walk. Alma knew it wasn't a good idea, but she went over to the Foam Hole over on Copper Creek, a beautiful secret known mostly only to local fisherman. A waterfall coming down into a sharp bend in the creek created a small white bubble bath of frothy water under the cool blue-green canopy of the ridge above. To the north of the Foam Hole, the wall of sheer rock extended several hundred yards, and there were caves big enough for a person to crawl into. Eva had let it slip one day about "going to the cave," and Alma knew that had to be where it was.

Ezra was sitting in the mouth of the cave behind some brush when he heard a horse snort. He froze and listened, then slowly reached for Father and Son. Leaning just slightly forward, he could see through a break in the branches of the bushes hiding the cave from the view of the creek that some fellow on a horse was riding down the creek.

Then the rider looked up, and Ezra saw that it wasn't a man at all, but Alma Newton! *What in the world is she doing? Is she looking for me?* Ezra's heart leaped at this thought, but then he realized that he couldn't let her know he was there. Somebody could be following her. She stopped then and climbed down from the horse. After looking around, she pulled something out of her pocket and stuck it in the forks of a tree at the water's edge.

After she and Diamond cleared the first curve in the trail away from the creek, Ezra watched and waited for what seemed like an eternity to see if anyone else might happen along or if she was coming back. Finally, Ezra climbed down from his perch, skipped over the rocks to the other side, grabbed the letter, and raced back to the cave. He opened the letter and was amazed that it held a tiny bit of her scent. It read:

I hope you find this and not some fisherman who just happens by. I want you to know two things. One is that everything will be all right. I don't know how I know these things, but I just do. If things weren't going to turn out right, I would feel it, but I don't. I know you're disappointed that your problem continues, but time takes care of us all. The second thing I want you to know is that I'm waiting for you. I would like to say more, but I don't want to be too specific. In case someone besides you finds this letter, I don't want it to make sense!! These words are for you and you only, as am I.

—Alma

Ezra stood up and slapped his leg and read the whole note again.

***

Alma awoke the next morning with her intuition stronger than ever that all would be well. She didn't put back on the man's clothes that upset her father so. She put on a nice dress and fixed her hair, and her father did a double-take and smiled when she came in for breakfast.

"Well, now, that's better." Sam grinned and sipped his coffee.

"I'm going to the store. Is it okay if I put some things on your account?"

"Sure, if you need something."

"Oh, I do." Alma smiled. "I need new clothes. I'm going to buy some new cloth. I heard they got some in down at the store, first time in months. I'm bound to have some before it gets gone."

"Women and their pretties." Sam said, trying to sound stern, but he was actually pleased. He kissed her on the cheek and went out of the house whistling a tune. Things were back to their normal routine, and he was happy.

Alma went into the store with the expectation of just getting some coffee and a couple of pieces of fabric and getting out quickly.

She hoped Mrs. Blevins wasn't there and immediately felt guilty for the thought. It was mostly old men who hung around there all the time. *Women don't have near enough hours in the day as it is, and if a woman did come in and sit, people would talk about how sorry and no-account she was.* So Mrs. Blevins wore loneliness like rouge and cornered any female who came in to ask about the gossip or to swap a recipe. She knew everything about everything in the community.

Alma stepped up to the counter; she heard the curtain over the door separating the store from the family living quarters swish and knew there would be no escaping now.

"Alma, how are you today? How's your daddy and them?"

"We're all fine, m'am. I came all the way down here yesterday and forgot to get coffee. Makes me so mad to do things like that. And I hear you've got cloth."

"Well," Mrs. Blevins gave Alma a funny look. "You've got a lot on your mind right now, I reckon. It's easy to forget things."

Alma knew she was referring to Ezra, and she felt her face start to flush a little. Mrs. Blevins took her over to the three bolts of cotton, and Alma liked all of them. As she waited for enough fabric from each one for a dress, she noticed that the men playing checkers in the corner had stopped talking and looked around at the sound of Alma's voice. Jacob Collier, an overbearing, red-faced man whose family would almost certainly have to hire pallbearers when he died, cleared his throat.

"Did y'all hear about all of them stores being broke into down in Alley Valley and up in Manville? They's been three of them hit."

Jacob stopped and spit a thick glob into a bottle he kept by his chair. "Might be some hobos coming through, or it may be some of these slackers, these crybabies who won't step up and do their duty. It might've even been that Teague boy they been looking for."

Alma gave Mr. Blevins the money when she had everything wrapped and ready to go, and he and his wife stood and stared blankly at Alma. "Thank you. Have a good day."

81

Alma just nodded and walked over to the checkerboard. She leaned over and took one of John Baker's checkers and skipped twice over two of Jacob's pieces, then placed the pieces in a stack in front of John. She looked levelly at Jacob.

"Ezra don't come from people who steal. And you know it."

She turned and walked away, the twirl of her skirt blowing the scent of her lavender soap into the open mouths of the surprised checker players.

EZRA'S JOURNAL

Feb. 1, 1919

I've got work to do. Even if I'm out of the really big trouble, they'd still likely put me in jail for a while or jerk me back up to Camp Lee for a while. So I'm going to get busy and cut Eva more firewood. They want people to quit using coal because they need it for factories. In the paper it said that the President is going to have to shut down all the factories for a few days so people can get enough coal to keep them alive during this deep freeze. They've got everybody having whole days without bread or meat because there's a shortage. What crops is out there ain't getting picked because most of the men are gone. They say cotton and sugar have gone sky high. This is so hard on the women. There's so many of them like Eva, alone, hungry, scared, cold, their men off someplace they never heard of.

Revelations

The book of Revelations is just about the strangest thing I ever read. Preachers refer to it all the time, but I don't remember ever studying it in church or Bible school. Now that I've read it, I can see why. It would scare a youngun to death.

In chapter 13, it says that a beast with seven heads and ten horns will rise up out of the sea and that it will wear a crown on each horn. And there is a dragon supposed to come, too. But angels come down and fight with them, and then John the Revelator tells that Jesus says "Behold I come quickly." I just don't know what to make of it all.

There is only one thing I can say for sure about it—if there is dragons and seven-head monsters rising up out of the sea, I probably wouldn't be around to see Jesus come—I'd be dead along with just about everybody else from fright. I heard a preacher at a revival talking about how the war over in Europe was a sign of the beginning of the final judgment. With no way to know till it all happens, I just try not to think about it. I ain't going to read Revelations no more right now. I've got enough on my mind as it is.

Eva left me another note at the rock over at Hale Springs begging me to give up and come in. She said that there was a notice in the newspapers saying that the Army was going to go easy on deserters. They said if people would come in voluntarily, that they would have their cases heard by their local draft boards and would lean toward sympathy, but if they didn't come in on their own, they would publish their names in the papers as deserters. Eva don't want that to happen and I don't either. I can just see it now, the headline in the paper: NAMES OF LOCAL DESERTERS. I'm so glad Momma's not around to see it. But on the other hand, how do I know the article isn't a trick? They might just be fooling with us, telling us to come on in and everything will be all right, and then they'll be a picture of a bunch of people hanging from the gallows somewhere up at Fort Lee or Fort Knox. I don't know what to do. I just can't think about any of it any more, not Revelations, not Eva, not the newspaper. I'm going to go to the cave and take a long nap.

Feb. 1919

I just got another note from Eva. A soldier came to the house, a fellow named Nettles, and near scared her to death. He said my troubles ain't over by a long shot. I can't write no more right now, Book. What is there to say? I can't see no way out of this sorry mess except dying, and I ain't ready for that yet. I guess instead of writing, I better be doing some serious praying and studying.

But there is some good news, Book. I got a letter from Alma. She rode out here dressed like a boy and give me a real scare till I seen who it was. She left me a letter in a tree saying everything was going to be all right and that she would be waiting for me. I couldn't hardly believe it. My eyes have done about wore the ink off the paper reading her words over and over. It's too good to be true.

<u>February Thaw, 1919</u>

I've started trying my hand at mapmaking. I don't have Eva's hand with a pencil, but I figure this will be useful later on. I've been in country I ain't never seen before. I've found some really good fishing holes and places to hunt. I've found big stands of holly bushes that I can cut from and maybe sell in town at Christmas time if I ever get out of this mess. I've found ginseng patches and blackberry patches and all kinds of useful stuff. Knowing how my mind is getting, I'll never remember it all later if I don't put it on paper somewhere.

I liked geography in school. Miss Jeter, my teacher, had a globe and a big map that I never got tired of. She told us all about countries and mountains like ours. She said that our mountains were baby mountains. It was hard to believe. Some of these mountains, especially up on High Knob, are so high it's scary to look off of them. But she said even in our own country there are mountains much higher. Out west people would probably call our mountains hills she said. And in other parts of the world there are mountains way taller than the ones out West. I could not imagine it.

She also explained about our local geography. I had always noticed that whenever we had a big snowstorm in the winter, some people would come to church saying they had snow up to their boot tops, and others would say it was almost knee deep at their house. Miss Jeter said that was because Scott County was at the end of the mountains and some of the land was lower, some of it was pretty high up. She said that the higher up you are, the heavier the snow, and the colder the air. She said that if you were to go up high enough in the air, even in the summer time you would freeze to death. I couldn't understand why it wouldn't get hotter since you were getting closer to the sun, but I kept quiet. I never did ask too many questions. Dad always said it's better to keep quiet and be thought a fool than to open your mouth and remove all doubt.

Hoping for Spring 1919

I don't see how Eva has made it. It seems there's a shortage of everything. Food is scarcer and more expensive than it used to be. Even the restaurants around have quit serving bread since it's so hard to get wheat. And I heard somebody coming out of Starnes store complaining about how high cloth was getting, said we'd all have to go back to wearing hides like the Indians used to, if this keeps up. And then with the coal miners striking and the factories needing so much coal, and bad weather, too, nobody can get coal.

At least I can help Eva with that. I've been chopping up every old snag I can find and leaving her notes in the smokehouse about where to go get it. It's harder to heat with just wood because it won't last as long, and you have to get up during the night to tend the fire or you'll freeze. Maybe the coal miners will get back to work soon or the war will get over or something will happen that will make it a little easier on folks. I don't see how they can stand much more.

And to beat it all, they're fixing to outlaw liquor, too. All of it. During the hardest times anybody can remember, with people having a reason to need a little drink. Now I understand why people have bad feelings toward the stuff, Lord knows. I've seen firsthand the fights and accidents and so forth that it leads to sometimes. But outlawing it all at once just means that people are going to sneak around. I've already accidentally run upon two stills used for making moonshine, and I got out of there in a hurry! For somebody like me, it's bad news in all directions. The people who's making it sure don't want anybody to find their still, partly because they fear somebody ratting on them to the law, but even more they fear some of these old boys showing up to take some free whiskey. And then, too, now that it's getting illegal, the government has got special whiskey agents on the hunt of people making and selling illegally. Them fellows might not take time out from their work to collar a soldier on the run like me, but I ain't taking no chances.

And I've decided something, Book: I ain't going in right now and give myself up. I just don't trust what they're saying, first of all, and I need to find a way to get Eva some money, too, before I go and maybe get locked up.

Spring 1919

Well, now I believe I have heard it all. There is a trash dump down along the creek below Papaws down there. People are all the time bringing stuff they don't know what to do with a leaving it there. It is a big mess. Anywhere there's trash like that you find rats. Well, I was walking through there yesterday morning. It was real early and that being way back like it is, I wasn't even looking around for anybody, but I heard voices as I started down the hill, and before I had time to hide or anything, a little boy stepped out just a few yards ahead of me from some tall grass. He had the biggest old wharf rat you ever saw by the tail, it was dead. He hollered "Look at this," and another little boy stepped out. "There you go, Roy," he said, "that'll get us some money." I had to ask. What do you mean money? They didn't even look surprised or anything that I was there. You know how kids is when they get excited. They mighta thought I was there for the same reason as them. "We's killing rats for the contest," the little blonde one said, "but don't you tell."

I told him I didn't even know what he was talking about, and then he told me. He said that Kingsport was sponsoring a contest to pay money for every dead rat that was brought into City Hall. I thought he was lying to me for sure, but the older one spoke up and said, "That's right. They's crawling in rats over there, and they want to get rid of them so they put a bounty on them like they did bobcats one time. Only that's too far for us to go, so we kill 'em here and send 'em over there by our uncle. They don't know the difference." I told 'em I wouldn't tell nobody and to be careful. That beat anything. The government payin' for rats. And them younguns being smart enough to think up how to get in on it. It tickled me.

Spring 1919

The old ones, the Cherokee, named this place Devil's Fork, high in the Laurel Hell of Stone Mountain, an underserved name for such a beautiful place. Furious fast water comes from two directions off Powell Mountain and bounds over boulders big as cows in a white roaring foam. I was sitting on one of them, lost in the roar, thinking about Adam and Eve in the garden, I swear, when I caught sight of a blur to my right. Right then and there,

I turned to see the biggest rattler I'd ever seen. It was just like my thoughts had conjured up the very serpent Satan himself. I wanted those rattlers so I picked up the biggest rock I could lift and smashed it. It struck at me twice with that terrible tongue darting in and out.

But he'll not be scaring anybody else that way. I've got those nine rattles and a button back in the cave. When I held him up by his tail, he was almost as long as me, so he must have been close to six feet. It just goes to show that no matter how beautiful this earthly paradise is, there's still snakes in the garden.

Beekeeping

I find myself going back up to the Rollins Swamp again and again. Today was my best trip ever. I decided to just keep walking when I got up there and see what's on the other side. I saw a flock of wild turkeys and some deer. But the last thing I expected to see all the way up there was a man, but there he was. Like to scared me to death. I heard somebody cough, and I froze. I couldn't see anything at first, and I thought I might be got for sure. But then I caught a wisp of smoke. Who could this be? Another outlaw. I crept closer and closer, but staying upwind. I watched where I stepped and didn't make much noise at all. Then I could see that it was a man and he was tending bees! There must have been 10 stands in there. There's nothing more interesting than bees. My daddy had a few stands when he was young. When I's little, he'd let me hold the smoker while he'd rob the honey.

A man can learn a lot from bees. Every bee in the hive has a specific job, and he don't shy away from it. The queen is in charge of everything. She not only makes the baby bees to keep the hive going, but she is necessary to even have a hive at all. And she won't tolerate another female coming into her business either. I've heard fellows talk about how jealous women is, how after you get married you're under a 'petticoat government.' That's just nature's way. Personally it don't sound too bad to me, this petticoat government, if it was the right petticoat.

Summer 1919

This has been one more long, hot, dry summer. It seems like I've just got used to living like this. Sometimes I go for hours and hours when I don't even think about this whole mess, or about my old life, or about the future. The days just stretch into a bright blur one after the other.

I get tired—that ain't changed. I walk so much that a lot of nights I dream I'm walking all night long and wake up wore out. But even so, I'd have to say that this has been one of the best summers of my whole life.

In a way I feel more alive than I ever have been. The sounds of the bees and birds and bugs are sharper and clearer than I ever remember, and a new quiet place has opened up inside of me that I never had before. Maybe I'm just now really growing up, which strikes me as kind of funny as I write it. I may be growing up, but I'm getting smaller. I've lost so much weight that I can't hardly keep my pants up. I had to go into somebody's barn yesterday and cut a piece of twine off a haybale and tie my pants up tight around me. My hipbones stick out like a poor cow's. I've just walked my hind end off.

Ginseng Hunting

I've had a good day, but tiring. I walked all the way up to Rollins Swamp looking for sang. I need to take Eva some money before I go in and maybe get locked up. It was a long hard climb up there. I knew I was really getting into some good country when I caught wind of the cool musky smell, the smell of wet earth and heavy cover. I remember seeing some 'sang up there a couple of years ago when Judge Hilton took me up there looking for grouse. But I couldn't remember exactly where we went, so I just cut the top of the knob up into garden size squares and stepped it off just like I's laying out planting rows. I'd been walking a good hour or so and finally set down under a big poplar to catch my breath, looked over, and there it was, a big patch of 'sang. Those little pointy tip leaves were all over that little spot, just shiny and pretty as a new penny and with those bright red berries on a lot of them.

I dug and dug those roots until I was wore out. Had a knapsack stuffed full. Boy, Eva would be tickled. She could take it to old man Starnes down at the store, and he'd pay her whatever the going rate was. They say that he ships that stuff down the river from Kingsport to Chattanooga, then they take it on to Philadelphia to ship over to them Chinese. I've never tried any of it myself, but they say it makes a tea, and them Chinese use it to make themselves stronger and healthier. Jed Harper told the men down at the store that he heard the men over there used it so they'd be able to 'stay in the saddle' longer, but I don't believe that. Jed is always going on with some foolishness to make your face turn red.

I can't remember if I wrote about it or not, I don't believe I did. I found some sang a few days ago. It wasn't much, but it's money. And wouldn't you know it? I was crossing the creek over on Charlie Quillen's place and a bird flew right by my head so I had to dodge real fast. My foot slipped and next thing I knowed, I was sitting in the creek, with a durn raincrow sitting up in a tree laughing at me. I lost hold of the 'sang, so I just let it float on down and went for a swim.

Thinking

I need to try to tell you about yesterday, but I don't know if I can. I was reading the Psalms trying to get sleepy, and I came to 139 where it said "If I rise on the wings of the dawn, if I settle on the far side of the sea, even there your hand will guide me."

In Romans, it says that people really don't know how to pray but that the spirit can speak without words. I climbed on up to that big rock jutting out over the creek, feeling sleepy, sat down, and closed my eyes. I was going to pray for a long time about everybody and everything, but I couldn't think what to say after a while, so I stopped. I fought my mind, fought to keep words out completely.

To keep your mind blank and still is impossible, but I finally did manage for just a few seconds to keep all the words out. I still saw stuff——Momma and Eva, Alma, just different pictures——but finally when I got the words shut off long enough that the pictures left too, and I saw this point of light. It was the strangest thing. I had this feeling like I wasn't here anymore. I didn't feel my legs or the wind or the heat as the sun came out from behind the clouds. I could hear my heart in my ears and see a little candle flicker in my head and that was it. But then the words came back and broke the spell. "I rise on the wings of dawn." I'm going to try it again and see if I can stay in there in that quiet place with the little light for a longer time.

Honey Locust Thorns

I was walking along paying no attention and let one of those branches pierce my shoulder. When I seen what it was, I felt sick to my stomach. The only thing that'll hurt any worse for any longer is a snake bite. They say that they're meant to remind us of what Christ went through on the cross with that crown of thorns, and I think they do a mighty good job. I deserved to run into it because, as usual, I was gawking along looking up at the sky, trying to take in how many walnuts there was. The trees were as full as grapevines. There's a lot of chestnuts, too, and I decided I could go to Homer McDavid's and get me a grain sack out of his barn to fill up. Eva can pass a day or two taking a hammer and smashing all those up for pies and cakes.

While I was in the barn, I found some salve for the cow's tits, and I rubbed some of that on my shoulder. *I hope I don't grow a nipple there*, I thought to myself and wished there was somebody there I could say it to and make them laugh with me. I said it out loud anyway just to hear it.

Chapter 13

The Second Year Begins

October 1919

EZRA & PARSONS'S WIFE

As the second fall in the woods began, Ezra was beginning to feel the strain of the long solitary journey. His checks were hollow and chapped, his lips swollen and cracked, but the greatest change was in his eyes. Those who had seen him mentioned in whispers to each other that he looked like he might be 'goin' off' a little, that the fear and cold and hunger were starting to get to him.

Ezra knew himself that he was wearing down. A look at his reflection in the creek alarmed him, too. And now there was a cough. It had started just as a little runny nose and scratchy throat. He thought a little salve and some hot whiskey would fix him right up.

He knew Eva had the salve they had made a year ago. Their grandma had taught them how. Eva had sent him all around

Stoney Creek until he found a Balm of Gilead tree. She sang gospel songs he remembered as he worked on stripping the bark. The closest farm with some sheep was several miles away, and the day-long walk to go and borrow some mutton's tallow to cook the bark in left him so tired and weak that he thought he would need to use some of the salve right then. By the time Eva got the whole concoction boiled down into a smelly ooze in his iron skillet, Ezra was sick of the smell and swore he'd never use the stuff, no matter how sick he was. But right now, he'd give anything for some on his chest, followed by a big cup of hot whiskey and a long, deep sleep.

After he ate a little breakfast, he felt sick, and his legs felt like fence posts. *I've got to lay down somewheres. If somebody finds me or I die, that'll just be it.* He crawled underneath some bushes and curled up on his side. Almost instantly, he fell asleep. When he woke up, he realized his nose was against something warm, fuzzy, leather-smelling. In terror he realized he was across a horse and was too weak to do anything about it. Suddenly a hand appeared on his forehead.

"He's awake. Stop just a minute, George."

Ezra looked up into a blurry face gradually coming into focus. It was Elizabeth Osborne, the preacher's wife.

"Lay still, Mr. Teague. You've got a high fever. We're taking you home."

Ezra thought she meant she was taking him to Eva, and he wanted to protest. "I've been enough trouble to Eva," he mumbled. *Besides, those Army men would find me there. Maybe that's the best. It's over; I'm probably dying anyway.* He drifted off to a delirious half-sleep.

When he opened his eyes again, he realized he was not at home, and this was not Eva bending over him studying his face. He was lying on a blanket in the hay, a cow staring at him over the stall, chewing. Mrs. Osborne was putting a cold cloth on his head. He tried to get up, but she pushed on his chest hard enough to surprise him.

"Lay down unless you aim to die."

Ezra was surprised again. The tone of voice was angry, used to being obeyed.

"You're really sick. You've probably got pneumonia. You can stay in here until you get better."

She turned then, skirts flying, and hurried out. Ezra was still disoriented and weak. The smell of something good drew him up on one side; it was potato soup with a strong onion smell. Ezra lapped it up like a starved hound and fell back into the hay exhausted.

By the next day Ezra tried to stand and found his legs weak and unsteady. Afraid to show himself, he peeped around the barn door to get his bearings. He was at the back of the parson's house. The house faced the road, and there were two steep hillsides that rose up on each side of the house. Ezra realized that the only way someone could see him would be from inside the house or if they were climbing around the sides of those steep hillsides. He relaxed a little.

Just then the back door flung open and here came Mrs. Osborne at a quick clip. She was carrying something in a basket, and Ezra hoped it was something to eat. The wind was howling today, and it blew her hair across her eyes and whipped her skirts between her legs until it was hard to walk. The parson stepped out on the porch then and called to her. The wind took his words away, but Mrs. Osborne stopped and turned around. The parson walked out to her then, and they had a conversation.

Ezra could hear nothing they said, although they were only 20 yards or so away. Their mouths moved, they gestured with their hands, their faces were intense. Ezra imagined the words floating away spinning, spiraling like oak leaves, and sticking in the trees on the hillside. Mrs. Osborne turned to walk away, but the parson grabbed her by the arm and spun her around. Ezra realized then that they were arguing about something. Was it him?

When Mrs. Osborne stepped into the barn, she was startled to find Ezra standing up and right in her face as she turned the corner. Her hair was down in strings from the wind, and her face was red.

"Oh, you're better." Ezra thought she sounded a little sad about that, which was puzzling.

"Yes m'am. I want to thank you for what you done."

"We had no choice. My husband found you out there near dead. Here's some hot biscuits." There was a hardness in her voice, and Ezra felt confused. He ran over to the quilt and sat down, unwrapping the biscuits as he went. He ate quickly.

"My husband says you need to leave. If the Army men find you here, he says, we could be in real trouble." She turned to stare at him again.

"Yes m'am. I'm going."

"No, you're not. You're too sick. You won't make it another month out there now that it's winter and your lungs is bad. He says he's prayed about it, and God says you need to move on now, turn yourself in. Well, I've prayed about it, and God spoke to me about helping you. I reckon God must be trying to figure it all out, too."

For the first time, Ezra saw a just a little hint of a grin on her face. He couldn't help but grin, too, and nod at her. She went back in the house then, and Ezra knew he'd found a safe place to winter.

<u>EZRA'S JOURNAL</u>

<u>Sickness</u>

Eva keeps writing notes to me saying I should come in and stop this scouting around, but I'm not going anywhere right now. I'm just too sick, and I don't want to take a chance on giving it to anybody. It may be that deadly flu everybody's got. I'm just too sick to write any more right now. I've got to lay down.

<u>September 1919</u>

I don't know why the Osbornes are helping me this way. It could get them in trouble. But I'm just too weak and heartsick to argue with them like I ought to. I'm feeling much better now. Mrs. Osborne has fed me good beans and soup and cornbread and fresh buttermilk. I'm ashamed at how much I ate these last two days. I'm going to pay them back when I get out of this; in the meantime, when I get to feeling better, I'll start bringing them a mess of trout every week.

The preacher's wife is a fine woman. But I get a funny feeling when I'm around her. The way she looks at me, sort of sad and like she wants to say something but doesn't. It must get lonely out here for her. She's from the city somewhere, I want to say. She seemed different when she first came here, but now she's just kind of quiet and sad. I hope me being here don't cause trouble between her and the preacher. I sure don't want no hard feelings between us because I need prayer, and I'll need the parson to either marry me or bury me when this mess is over.

Fall 1919

I'm so thankful to be here at the Osborne's. It's so cold I have to stay down under the hay. Cold weather's come awful early this year, or else my old bones are starting to suffer from this time sleeping on the ground. The preacher's been kind enough to leave several of his cattle in here, and they help warm it up. I can stand the smell better than freezing. Mrs. Bellamy brings me the newspaper, and I read every inch of it, even the little ads people put in about stuff for sale and community news and so forth. It takes about all afternoon. There was a funny one in there. Some fellow offered a description of his stolen hat and then wrote I CAN LICK THE MAN WHO STOLE MY HAT. Now how does he think the man who stole it will bring it back just to get a whipping?

He better think twice about advertising for a fight——I know that from experience. I used to beat up on the bigger guys at school who would be mean to the girls or the littler ones, but I got hurt a lot in the time of it. Because I wasn't too big, I had to learn to use my size and my quickness. And I had to learn to fight dirty. I would pretend I was giving up and walking away, then I would turn and hop down and sweep their feet out from under them with my leg. As soon as I had them on the ground, I'd gut punch them or hit them between the legs. Boy, that gets people madder than anything, but they hurt so bad they can't get up, and you get to run away and laugh at getting in the last lick.

One really sad thing I read in the paper said a man down at Possum Creek asked his wife to sing *Will You Miss Me* and then went out and hung himself in the barn. He had got the letter and the questions they send out to everybody they want for the Army, and I reckon he just couldn't stand the thought of it. The newspapers is full of bad news now of the local boys dying at the front and even more of them dying at the army camps from pneumonia and flu. The odds don't sound too good. You can die in your bunk at Camp Lee or Camp Oglethorpe or somewheres shaking with fever or you can ride on one of them big ships across the ocean and get shot up in Germany or somewhere. Not too good. Maybe it was God's will to make me run away. I can't get the words to that song out of my head now. "When death shall close these eyelids and this heart shall cease to beat. When I'm cold and still in my death, will you miss me when I'm gone?"

Newspaper

I keep thinking about some more of that stuff I read in the paper. It took me a while to go to sleep last night. They just seems to be lots of crazy stuff going on in the world. There's a bunch of people happy to outlaw liquor. Now it seems to me that whiskey does cause a lot of trouble—it sure leads to a lot of fights and killing, causes troubles between husbands and wives some times. But to outlaw it would be hard. It seems to me that it would be like trying to outlaw gossip, or jealousy—folks will just do it anyway. You can pass a law against anything you want to—cornbread, hunting dogs, pocket knives—but people are gonna go on and do what comes natural. I don't know what'll come of it, probably nothing.

The other thing in the paper that really stumped me is that they said that a bunch of women and some politicians are wanting to give women the right to vote. Imagine that, Eva voting. I can't. Eva don't know or care nothing about politics. She'd probably just ask me or some of the rest of the family who to vote for, and of course, we'd just tell her the names of Democrats. Nobody around here votes Republican except the blacks and some of the people who've moved in here from other places and a few whose family have always voted republican since the War Between the States because they didn't like the Confederacy and its army.

So maybe giving women the right to vote would be a good thing that would help the Democrats. That might not be so bad. But I just can't imagine the women I know wanting to vote; they like to talk about other stuff and probably wouldn't go vote it you let them.

Chapter 14

EZRA COMES IN

One early February morning, Ezra awoke in the barn to a feeling of warmth, energy, and hopefulness. It was unseasonably warm outside, and he cracked the barn door to drink in the air. He felt strong, his legs having a spring in them he hadn't felt in a long while. When Mrs. Osborne came out toward the barn with her egg basket, which he knew contained his breakfast, he opened the door for her, grinned, and bowed from the waist as she came through the door. She gave him a strange look for a moment; then she smiled back at him.

"Well, you're certainly feeling better." she said. "Your color looks the best I've seen since you came."

"Yes m'am, It's the fine cookin'," Ezra reached for the basket. "I think I've been enough trouble to you and the preacher. I best move on now, but I'll surely miss this." He smiled down at the biscuits, bacon, and fried potatoes in the basket.

Mrs. Osborne had a little frown, and her mouth drawn into a straight line. "I'm not sure that's such a good idea, Mr. Teague. If you get caught—"

Ezra looked a little surprised. There was a real fear in her voice; it reminded him of Eva.

"There's a reward now. In these hard times, somebody might just go for it," she said. She looked like she was going to continue, but she stopped herself. Ezra figured that she was right, but he didn't let it show on his face.

"I'll be alright." Ezra smiled and stood up. "Don't you worry no more about me. You've done enough. I've got a plan." He reached toward the empty basket, and she stepped closer to him, taking hold of the basket. She looked down at their almost touching hands. Ezra let go and stepped back. "I can't thank you or the preacher enough for what you've done for me. I won't forget it, or the debt I owe you."

"You don't owe me anything, Mr. Teague. I've enjoyed taking care of you."

She started through the door and then stopped to turn back. "You won't be here when I come back, will you?"

Ezra felt confused by the look on her face, the turn in her voice. He didn't know what to say, so he just nodded. He watched her all the way back into the house, and then he gathered up his things. He left the Osbornes a note promising fresh turkey come spring and more payback once he could get a chance to earn some money.

He watched the woods around the house for a long while, seeing if he might detect any movement or sounds. Satisfied that no one was out there, he slipped out the door, went around back of the barn, and both climbed and slid down a steep embankment. Ezra moved slowly, cautiously, not making any noise, making his way back across the ridge toward the caves.

He returned to the woods rested but weak, quieter, heavier, lonelier than he'd been before he got sick. His time with the Osbornes had just made him more homesick—or people-sick, really—made him long for home worse than ever. Ezra knew he had to find a way out of this mess he was in.

When he told the parson's wife he had a plan, he wasn't telling the whole truth. His only plan so far was to make a plan to stop running. Ezra really had no idea how to go about it. His first thought was to get Sam Newton and others in the community to help him. The fact that the preacher had been willing to take such a risk to help him was a good sign, he thought.

But Ezra had learned caution, if nothing else, during his months in the woods. He wanted more information before he made such a drastic step as he was contemplating. He started creeping closer to civilization to observe and, more importantly, to hear people talk.

One night he crawled up onto a pile of fresh sawed pine boards down at Dockery's Sawmill just as the men were cleaning up and going home. He listened to the banter until they were all gone and then he tried to remember everything to write it in his journal. He had finally fallen asleep, his arms crossed on his chest with a gun in each hand. When the mill hands reported for work the next morning, one had spotted him and quietly climbed up the stack to take a look. When he saw it was Ezra and Father and Son, he slipped back down the way one might retreat from a rattlesnake. All the men sat down on some stumps, rolled cigarettes, and waited for Ezra to wake up.

When Ezra finally did crawl down, he felt sort of sheepish and embarrassed. He rubbed his eyes and looked at them. No one spoke. He nodded at them, longing to say something, to hear their questions, to tell them about the bobcat he'd seen the night before, about the big timber rattler he killed, to ask them about their mothers, children, everyone. But Ezra and the men in the circle just stared at each other. Some of them looked at him sadly, and Ezra saw that they felt sorry for him. So he had simply nodded again and walked away. As the sun danced through the poplars and the heat shimmered along the fields, he climbed back toward Stone Mountain, up to another cave he knew. He spent a good part of the day reading his Bible. It was that day's scripture and the look on those millhands' faces and the ache he felt almost all the time now in his chest that had led him to do something so risky as to go to Wayland again and crawl back under the church.

Ezra got up with the sun and walked quickly to the rocky hillside behind the church. Still weak from his bout with pneumonia, he had to stop and rest a minute after he made the climb up to the back of the church. He returned to the same comfortable spot he'd used before where he could see through the little knothole in the floor. He lay contented, even dozing, with the music of the hymns drifting in and out of his consciousness, and he smiled in his sleep. When church was over, people stood out in the yard and visited for at least 30 more minutes. Ezra roused at the sound of voices; he knew he could get caught up on some of the community news this way. Polly Baker had her baby, another boy. The Depews were buying some more land on Lick Creek. James Stewart and Lucy Jones were getting married. After everyone else had left, there were only two men left behind still talking. One of the men was Samuel Newton, Alma's father, and the other was Jack Flanary, the richest landowner in the community and a county leader. Ezra stopped breathing and strained to hear what they were saying when he caught the sound of his own name.

"Well, I just think somebody's got to do something, Sam, because otherwise there could be bad trouble."

"It wouldn't be right to turn him in, Jack. I won't be a party to it."

"I ain't saying that. But somebody needs to convince him to come in. This place is crawlin' with those smart-aleck Army people asking questions, snoopin' into everything, and everybody hates it.

You know what a predicament this is, now. The Home Guard's not in the business of helping the Feds, especially to punish a man for doing what he ought to, but they don't want these boys in here watching everybody either. All these shirkers need to come in now."

Newton spat a circle in the soft swept dirt of the church yard not six feet from where Ezra lay under the church as he spoke.

"It would be better if Ezra gave himself up; things would go easier for him maybe. If we could get word to him somehow that we'll all speak for him, the sheriff, the judge, myself, and he won't do much time maybe—"

Newton and Flanary stood quietly, and Ezra thought that they would surely hear the loud thud of his heart and his quick breathing and drag him out from under the church. The two men began walking away toward their horses then, and Ezra couldn't make out their words. He lay there for a long time, his mind a jumble. They were right, he knew. It would go easier on him if he surrendered on his own. And he knew they were probably right about the increasing concern among the Home Guard and the community, for that matter. It made sense.

With a single sheriff on horseback, 538 square miles of mountainous land, and a scattered population, the county had law and order only through self-policing and a strict code of conduct. Having soldiers hunting for people was too much a reminder of the past the Scott Countians would rather forget. Since the time of the Civil War when everyone from the Confederate Army itself to its deserters to the Union soldiers had plundered and pillaged throughout the area, the local people often organized themselves to keep order. Their justice was swift, and penalties for breaking God's and man's law were severe. Anyone caught stealing from a neighbor would have his home burned to the ground so he would have to move on. A man who beat his wife or kids would find a pile of sticks on his front porch when he started out for his daily chores—a kind of calling card of warning that any further bad behavior would be punished.

These people believed in taking care of their own problems. The government had urged communities to form citizen militias since the National Guard had been called up, and here in remote southwest Virginia, it was already loosely organized, since a remnant of these Home Guards had continued to operate, although less so than in the past. Ezra knew his predicament was creating exactly the kind of outside attention that many folks here feared and hated and that the patience and the protection of his neighbors would eventually run out. *They're right. They are, and I know it. This is crazy. I can't keep on.*

When all the sounds of voices and scuffling feet and horses finally stopped, Ezra cautiously crawled out of his hiding place and walked slowly back toward the caves. His heart was heavier than ever. *I thought church would make me feel better,* he said to himself, *but I never thought I'd hear anybody talking about me that way.*

At the Hale Springs where Eva left his ammunition, Ezra found his Army uniform all clean again, pressed and folded, still lying on a quilt she had wrapped it in with a dogwood branch laid over it for cover. He had left it in the smokehouse under some old grain sacks for Eva, and, of course, she had gotten it done and returned to him right away. *Good, sweet Eva.* Ezra smiled at the thought of her. *She deserves so much better than she's got.*

The uniform looked like it had shrunk a little but it still fit. He took it back off and got in the creek to wash off. When he got dressed again, he looked at this reflection in the water. The man who stared back at him looked scary, wild, and sickly, but Ezra smiled at him anyway and set off to talk to the one person who could help him. When he crossed the ridge and saw the big white house, he stopped for a minute to get up his nerve and to say a little prayer. *If I'm wrong about him, then this is the end of the road for me. Once I go down there and show myself to him, they'll be no turning back.* Ezra took a deep breath and set off down the hill.

EZRA'S JOURNAL

Winter 1920

I know what I must do; I need somebody to vouch for me—I need to go talk to Alma's daddy, but something keeps holding me back. But I can't seem to get my nerve up. I've been watching the Newton house for 2 nights now, trying to get some idea of how to go about approaching Sam Newton. What I saw last night has got me ashamed to go down and try to look him in the eye.

I was watching from the back of the house this time, the side facing the mountain. I guess Alma didn't feel any need to close her curtain because of that, or maybe she was just thinking of something and wasn't paying attention. But anyway, she came into the room and got ready for bed right in front of me. She unfastened her hair and it came down to the middle of her back. She wore a very loose cotton slip. When she lifted her arms to comb her hair, I could see her breasts and belly and the soft light shone through the slip to reveal the whole glorious shape of her. I lost my breath almost, and my heart beat so loud I thought she'd hear me.

I turned away, ashamed of myself, and walked straight back to the cave. I tried to read my Bible and pray for my lustful thoughts, but I couldn't get the picture of her out of my mind long enough to concentrate.

Then as I was fumbling around, my thumb fell into the Song of Solomon. I couldn't believe what I was reading. "I am my beloved's, my beloved is mine. O prince's daughter! The joints of thy thighs are like jewels, the work of the hands of a cunning workman. Thy naval is like a round goblet, thy belly is like a heap of wheat set about with lilies. Thy stature is like to a palm tree, and thy breasts are to clusters of grapes. I said I will go up to the palm tree, I will take hold of the boughs thereof: now also thy breasts shall be as clusters of the vine, and the smell of thy nose like apples; and the roof of thy mouth like the best wine for my beloved, that goeth down sweetly, causing the lips of those that are asleep to speak." And so on.

I couldn't believe my eyes, such talk in the Bible. But I've been thinking about it. How could such beauty be an accident? How could such a powerful feeling be wrong or a mistake? No, God doesn't make mistakes. So Solomon is just talking about a natural wonder of creation.

That's why I've got to get out of this mess somehow. I've got to have something to offer Alma and be able to walk up to her, look her in the eye, and tell her I love her.

Alma

I can't stop thinking about Alma now ever since I saw her in that slip. I've been having dreams about her that I can't even tell you about, Book. I'm afraid somebody might read it and go tell her, and then it would be all over before it started. But let's just say that the dreams are so sweet I've been taking naps several times a day in hope of having one. Philippians says to only think on things that are pure, honest, lovely and so forth, and Alma is all those things. But when I'm asleep my minds just drifts over to doing things to her. I can't stop it, so I might as well enjoy it. When I'm awake I push those filthy ideas and pictures out of my head as soon as they come in. But I'm a weak man. I'm going to go sit on a warm rock now and see if I can take another nap.

1920

I hadn't really ever thought about it before, but what Sam Newton and Jack were talking about makes sense. The Home Guard probably ain't happy about me. They mainly try to keep order and to deep things quiet and peaceful.

I remember hearing Daddy talk about what it was like here in Scott County after the war. During the war, you couldn't get hardly anything at all——Addington's store was plumb empty. People bartered with one another and did without. After the war, it only got worse. They still wasn't enough supplies of any kind; the armies had done took a lot of the stock. To make it worse, they was all these thieves and scoundrels showed up to do just pretty much as they please, at least at first. They wasn't no law to speak of. That's how that Home Guard got started. Daddy says if some of the men hadn't got together and done something, he don't know what would have become of the place.

Anyway, the Home Guard people won't put up with the Army people or with these other bounty hunters running around making trouble. My good luck and good wishes from my neighbors may be fixing to come to a screeching halt. It's time to make a move.

Hoping for Spring 1920

The only thing keeping me going now is writing in the book, day-dreaming about Alma, and plunking on my old banjo. I've played till my fingers are sore. I play the old ballads mostly, the ones that have umpteen verses—that taxes my mind more, and I need that. One of the funny ones with many verses came to mind and I had to sit and write all the verses down to make sure I had it right. It's a funny one I heard my Grandpa sing called *The Preacher and the Bear.*

There's people that say such music is a sin, but I just don't under-stand how that could be. Sin is something that causes hurt to somebody. But music doesn't do anything but make people smile, clap their hands, and tap their foot. It's impossible to be sad when you're playing and singing. And just look at old man Hale's ghost coming back from the dead to play his banjo. Not that I've heard him or anything. I think people may just be making up that wild tale. But I will say this. I've been out here in these woods along Copper Creek for a good while now, and I've seen some strange things that I can't explain.

The other night just at dark I was walking through the Vermillion fields over to Hale Springs, and some rocks just started rolling off the bank above me on the path. I froze and crouched down, but I couldn't see, hear, or smell a thing. So I got up and walked real quiet. A little further on the path, some more rocks rolled down

111

right in front of me again. I saw these move! For no reason at all, they rolled off the bank and right down by my feet!

Now I wouldn't want nobody to know it, but all of a sudden, I felt a puff of cold air at the back of my neck, and the hair stood straight up on my arms, and I got out of there in a hurry. I ran off that hill, through the springs, and got out in the middle of the main road and walked. That's how spooked I was. The old ghost didn't bother me no more. He's kind of like me——he wasn't going to come out in the main road unless he just had to. I reckon he was satisfied, just wanting me to know he was there.

Chapter 15

EZRA APPEALS
FOR HELP

Samuel Newton was a man set in his ways. Alma knew that the exact routine would never vary. The strong black coffee and single boiled egg split down the middle for breakfast. More black coffee and some kind of fried meat for supper. His pipe and a book by the fire in winter, just the pipe out on the porch swing in warm weather.

It was fairly cool this night, but not fire-building weather yet. So Sam had just put on a jacket and taken his usual perch on the right side of the swing. He was lighting his pipe, lost in thought and time, and had no idea at all that anyone was around. When a voice said quietly, "Mr. Newton," Sam thought for a moment that he imagined it. Then Ezra spoke again, a little louder this time.

"Mr. Newton, it's Ezra Teague. I need to talk to you."

Sam thought he had better stay calm and not make any sudden moves. No telling what state of mind Ezra was in. He just kept smoking the pipe without turning around. He stopped swinging so the squeaking wouldn't drown out Ezra's soft voice. Sam didn't want him to speak loud enough to draw Alma out of the kitchen; he didn't want her involved in any way. Suddenly a little voice in his head said, "She's already involved," and the thought startled him, but Ezra was talking again, so he had to let it go.

"I'm tired of this scoutin', Mr. Newton and I'd like to stop. But I don't want to go to jail for stayin' with my mother while she was dyin'."

"I'm sympathetic to you, Ezra—everybody is. But why have you come to me?"

"Because you're an educated and smart man. And you've got connections. You'll know what to do."

"Well, desertion is serious business. They could charge you with treason. Do you understand that, Ezra? They could say you're a traitor to your country for deserting the uniform—"

"But I ain't."

Ezra's voice grew louder, more excited, and he stepped out of the shadow of the boxwoods at the edge of the porch into the light from the window.

"Nobody will say I did. I'm in uniform,"

Sam finally turned now to look at him. His hair was long and matted like a dog's, and his beard almost touched his chest. The baggy uniform hung on his skinny frame, and with his dark sunken eyes and all that wild hair, he looked like the garden scarecrow.

At that moment Alma stepped out the screen door and froze. She stared at Ezra in fear at first, then amazement as she recognized him.

"Ezra," she whispered, "is that you?"

Ezra nodded. "Don't be afraid, please. I come to say thank you and to talk to your dad."

"Thank you for what?" Alma said.

Ezra started to tell her how much he'd appreciated hearing her ask for prayer for him at church, but the he thought better of it. *I might not ought to tell her that I been hiding under the church like a rat. She'll think I've gone crazy out here.*

"Uh, for going to see Eva. She told me about how you come calling on her and being so nice and all. She gets awful lonely."

"You're welcome, Ezra." Alma then held his gaze with a softness and steadiness to it that made Samuel Newton uncomfortable. She looked at her father then for a long moment and stepped back into the house.

"What do you want me to do, Ezra?"

"I want you to take me in and then stick by me, speak on my behalf."

Sam knew that he had no choice. The look on Alma's face had told him that.

"Let me think about how to go about his, Ezra. Come back tomorrow evening, and I'll tell you what we're going to do."

Ezra nodded and said nothing for a minute. He thought about going up on the porch to shake Samuel Newton's hand, but then he thought he'd better not. He wanted to talk more but he didn't know what to say. He sensed Newton's tension and decided he better not linger.

"Thank you, sir. Thank you. I really appreciate anything you might do. I'll be back tomorrow night." Ezra stepped back behind the boxwood.

"That's good, son. I'll talk to some people—" Newton stood up thinking Ezra would still be in earshot, but to his surprise, he was nowhere to be seen. He stepped off the porch into the yard and went around the hedges to look. Nothing. He looked out toward the barn and then over to the pond and chicken coop. Ezra had just vanished. Newton scratched his head and chuckled to himself. *No wonder they haven't been able to catch him,* he thought.

Feeling like he was floating, like a 50-pound pack had been lifted from his back, Ezra set off across the ridge to Hale Springs. It must have been the distraction of thinking about surrendering, or maybe the distraction of that long silent look from Alma that caused Ezra to get careless.

He walked straight back down the creek to the cave near Hale Springs where he had been sleeping instead of circling in from the ridge above and making sure he was alone. He ran straight into trouble, walking with his head down, lost in thought, and the Army guys who jumped out of the thick undergrowth to grab him were amazed how easy it was, after all those months of heat, weariness, and frustration. As elated as Nettles was to finally have someone in custody, he felt real irritation that they hadn't even been looking for Ezra at that moment and that his capture had been totally a fortuitous accident. Of course, Nettles wasn't going to write it up that way. *I'll have to get Smith and Cooper straight on the details of what happened before we get to Gate City,* he thought.

They had Ezra mounted on a little horse with his hands tied behind him in a matter of minutes. Ezra was stunned and dejected at the quickness of it. The Army fellows were laughing and slapping each other on the back, talking about how they couldn't wait to be out of this "backwoods hellhole" and get back to civilization.

They camped for the night down along Copper Creek. Even though it was only about eight more miles to Gate City, they decided to wait for morning to take Ezra into town.

"I want these people to see him brought in with the hand-cuffs," Nettles told Mac. "It might discourage any more of these cowards from running from their duty."

Mac's face reddened a bit, but he said nothing. He went over and gave Ezra a piece of beef jerky and set a cup of water down beside him. The young cocky one with the wild hair called Cooper had taken the two nice pistols Ezra had and was admiring them. He stood up and pretended he was drawing them like a gunslinger in some Western picture show. Mac just shook his head. *These boys are such horse's asses. I don't know if I could stay in the Army with them, either.*

"That's my property, mister, and you better take care of them," Ezra looked levelly at Cooper, and there was a threatening edge to his voice.

"Well, you better shut up, and remember who's got who," Cooper grinned and got close to Ezra's face.

Mac shot a warning look at Nettles, as Ezra stirred like he was trying to get on his feet.

"Those were my daddy's when he was boy, and if anything happens to them, somebody's gonna answer for it. " Ezra's face was dark now.

"Give those to me, Private." Nettles stepped between the two.

"I'm not hurting them, Lieutenant. Let me kick his ass."

"I gave you an order. Go curry the horses."

Nettles took the pistols and put them in his pack. Throughout the confrontation, Mac hadn't taken his eyes off Nettles, and the lieutenant knew it.

"Your weapons will be secure, Mr. Teague. After this is all settled, they'll be returned to you or your family. Now I suggest everybody get some sleep."

Nettles went over to the edge of the clearing, almost out of the light of the campfire and climbed in his bedroll. In just a few minutes, he was asleep.

The other soldier kept watch as Ezra tried to settle down and nap himself, but his sleep was fitful. He dreamed of his mother and father, but not like they looked now. They were young and smiling, holding Eva and Becky, his baby sister who died from measles, by the hand. Then he dreamed that he was choking, like something was around his neck, and he woke up with his heart pounding. Ezra was relieved to see the pink fingers of the sun reaching up over the mountain so he could get up and stop thinking about everything.

He was so preoccupied with relief and elation that morning was almost here that he didn't notice a little pinpoint of firelight coming down the hill toward them. In the next instant, Mac and Nettles woke up and froze, not trusting their eyes, dumb and open-mouthed. In a few more seconds, the horses were almost on top of them as a group of men on horseback broke through the brush at a gallop and circled around them.

Ezra looked around the circle. Some of them wore cloth hoods that covered only their head, and he was sure he knew who a couple of them were. Several had on large pieces of cloth that covered their whole bodies with the eyeholes and armholes cut out. Everyone was silent, the only sound the labored breathing of the animals. One of the soldiers started to reach for his holster, but one of the horsemen shot out of the line and charged him, knocking him on his back on the musky forest floor.

"Don't try that again. Don't make us hurt you."

The voice growled in an attempt at disguise. In the dancing light of the torches, Ezra saw that none of the eyes in the hoods were looking at him. They were watching the soldiers. What would they do now? Would they take Ezra themselves, maybe knock the soldiers in the head? When two of them climbed down off the horses, Ezra tested the ropes on his hands, but they were rock hard. They grabbed him by his uniform, spun him around, and untied him.

"Get in there and stay."

One of them was pointing in the direction of the woods to his left, some of the toughest thickets in the whole area. Ezra started running and didn't look back until he got to the rock ledge.

Chapter 16

SAM AND ALMA GET INVOLVED

Sam Newton didn't sleep much that night after Ezra's visit. He'd sat on the porch and meditated through two pipes of tobacco. It wasn't that he had to decide whether to help Ezra or not: that had been decided on the spot. The question was how to go about it.

Sam wished more than anything that he could just give Ezra a bundle of money and a train ticket to some big city someplace where he could just disappear into the crowd. That would be the easiest solution. But Sam was ashamed of himself for thinking of it. Alma would never forgive him if he did that. Ezra would never go for it either. Staying close to his family was his motivation for getting into this mess in the first place.

Inside Alma was working in the kitchen. He heard the sound of pots falling, then Alma crying out, not in pain but in anger, and then the sound of her footsteps heavy and angry through the house. Her bedroom door slammed.

Sam paused in mid-puff and listened. Alma was not usually one of those emotional women, but she was upset today. When she had come out of the house earlier with a big plate of food for Ezra, she had been furious with Sam.

"Why did you let him leave? He should have come on in the house where it was warm. And I'm sure he's hungry. How could you?"

"I didn't even have time to think, Alma. He just disappeared like a fox."

She whirled back into the house and slammed the screen door.

What will I do if she starts crying? Sam thought. She hasn't done that since she was a very little girl. *Then I could just offer to take her fishing or let her have a nickel to go to the store for candy. It won't be that easy this time.*

Sam stood up and walked out to the end of the porch. His fields stretched out green and neat—to his left the cattle and to his right the horses, including two spring colts that still frolicked around their mothers. He scanned the tree line once more, hoping to see Ezra, hoping even more to not see him. *Maybe he'll go on in by himself, leave us out of it.*

If Alma hadn't gotten entangled in all this, Sam knew that his course of action would be clear. He would help Ezra any way he could, not only because he understood why he'd done what he did, but also because the community needed to get rid of this problem once and for all. But at that moment when Alma had stepped out that screen door, Sam had gotten the uneasy feeling that, once again, he was in the dark a little bit, just like the time that he was ready to punish Alma for sneaking off all the time, only to find out it was because she'd started her period and had questions for Mrs. Johnson, who sewed for her ever since Alma's mother died. Sam blushed at the memory of that time. Once again, something mysterious, something he didn't fully understand, was happening. Sam wished he could think of a way to help Ezra but keep Alma out of it and away from Ezra, but there wasn't one.

He chuckled at himself and sat back down in his rocker. Fathering a daughter alone was certainly not something he'd ever gotten used to. When Alma was little, it was easier; he just pretended she was a boy. Taught her to shoot, ride, and hunt with the best of them. Taught her to be content with silence most of time and only an occasional hug. A fishing trip or a bag of gumdrops wasn't going to distract her this time. That look in her eye when she was Ezra in the yard that night just kept coming back to Sam. He'd never seen that look before on her, but he recognized it. Alma's mother had looked at him that way, he remembered, when they first met. *Sara, do I need you now!* He thought. *You'd know what to do.*

As one hour passed, then another, Sam grew bored, so he walked out to the barn and started currying Diamond, enjoying the smell of the hay and the animals, smiling to himself. Sam figured Alma had probably started reading, or maybe she was in the kitchen whipping up something special for dessert if she was still awake. The thought made him put the currycomb away and head toward the back door, hoping to run into the smell of a delicious pie bubbling in the oven.

Instead, he did a double take as Alma's startled face met him at the screen door, peering out from under a big felt hat. She had blackened the bottom of her chin and jaws with dirt, and she was wearing two of his old shirts and a pair of riding pants he had been looking for. She had on her boots and an old jacket thrown over it all, despite the warm weather.

"Now just where do you think you're going like that?" Sam frowned and reached toward her arm.

Alma stepped back and her eyes were sharp. "Let me be. I've got something I've got to do."

"Don't be a fool, girl." Sam's voice was half angry, half pleading. "It's the middle of the night. Come back here right now! He'll be back tomorrow!"

"No, daddy, he looks awful. There's no reason he can't just stay here for a few days. Nobody would even think of us hiding him. I'm going after him."

Alma ran out toward the barn. Sam hesitated, wondering where she could be going. In the seconds he stood there bewildered, trying to decide what he should do, she was out of the barn on Diamond's back at full gallop.

By the time she got to the top of the ridge she was winded and so was the horse. *I can't run like this all the way over to the cave. Besides, I need to be quieter.* So she put Diamond in a smooth trot and moved along the trail back to the cave. Just after she dropped off the ridge toward Copper Creek, she came to a place in the trail where it was obvious there had been several horses moving around. There were clear tracks in the mud, good size twigs broken off bushes and leaves. Alma had a bad feeling about it. If it was Sheriff Carter or someone else who had nabbed Ezra, they would take him straight to Gate City. So Alma set out in that direction, not trotting now, but moving quietly.

It was pitch black now, and Alma knew it was dangerous to ride; she would have to either turn back home or find somewhere to stay the night pretty soon. *If I don't go home tonight, Daddy will be out of his mind with worry.* She was just about to give up and turn back when she saw in the distance just below Copper Creek bluff a flicker of light. A campfire. She got off Diamond and tied him to a tree. Then she began making her way on foot, silently the way her father had taught her to move when hunting, toward the light.

She watched from a little knoll above the creek and saw Ezra sitting, dejected, his hands tied, in the edge of the firelight. The men with him were not locals or sheriff's deputies. They had on Army uniforms! Alma's heart pounded, and part of her dinner came up in her throat. She shifted her weight and started to sit down to think what to do, but a twig she hadn't seen under the leaves snapped loudly. Alma froze, and the man sitting next to Ezra who wasn't wearing a uniform stood up and looked straight at her in the dark. Ezra looked up, too, and one of the Army men said something she couldn't hear. She held her breath. After a long minute, they seemed to think all was well and went back to what they had been doing.

I'm sorry, Daddy, I'm so sorry. I'm going to have to stay put for now.

The men put out their bedrolls and began to settle in for the night. Alma carefully moved back against a little sapling and propped herself up. One of the Army men had two pistols and was pretending to draw them like he was in a gunfight. Ezra stirred then and said something in an angry tone to the man. Alma tensed as another man with lots of buttons and stripes on his uniform stepped out of the shadows and took the guns away from the man. She slowly pulled her legs under her, ready to run in and create a distraction if Ezra seemed to be in danger. But the man said something that seemed to change the look on Ezra's face, and the younger man who had been playing with the guns moved out of sight. They all settled down then and slept some.

Alma napped, too, for what seemed like only a few minutes, but when she opened her eyes, there was the faint light over the ridge indicating that dawn was approaching. She was marveling at herself for sleeping so soundly and rubbing her eyes when she noticed what appeared to be moving lights coming down around the bluff. She rubbed her eyes again, thinking she was surely imagining it, when the shape of horses became clear in the torchlight. As Alma watched, a group of men on horseback with their faces disguised by either sacks with holes in them or bandanas tied around their faces thundered into the camp area with guns drawn on the soldiers.

Is this someone coming to rescue Ezra or to take him and collect the $50 reward themselves? Alma wondered as she broke into a run back toward Diamond. It took her a few minutes to get back to him, and she was so winded and weak from the run and from fear that her head was swimming a little. But she took off down the creek out of sight and sound of the campsite and thundered across the creek. She ran hard along the edge past a deep and rocky place in the creek. Then when she reached the sandy bar in the creek-bed, she plunged Diamond in to the knee-deep water. Out of the corner of her eye she saw the torch lights start back up the bluff, and she started to turn Diamond back out of the creek to go after them. *They've got him,* she thought. *They're taking him to Gate City to collect the reward.*

But before she could get Diamond directed that way, a noise in front of her drew her attention. She held her breath so she could hear better. Someone was coming down the creek toward her pretty fast. If it was the soldiers, she didn't want them to see her full in the face and take a chance of being recognized later. She pulled Diamond toward the bank and got out along the edge where the brush would help shield her. But the figure taking shape out of the twilight was one she recognized. It was Ezra! She plunged Diamond back in the creek and rode toward him. Ezra looked up in a panic as the horse and rider approached him at full gallop and turned and started clawing up the muddy bank trying to get out of the creek on solid ground.

"Ezra! It's me!" Alma yelled. "Get on!" Ezra looked at her bewildered for a minute and then grinned and shook his head. He climbed up on one of the big rocks at the water's edge, and Alma moved Diamond up beside it for him to hop on behind her.

"You beat anything I ever saw," he said, and wrapped his arms around her waist.

Meanwhile, Sam had ridden all the way to the Teagues. Not finding any sign of Ezra or Alma, he went back home, thinking they would show up any minute. When the night dragged on and they weren't there, Sam paced the porch and the front room, smoking his pipe. *Alma's got sense. She must have taken him to Mrs. Johnson's or maybe they went on in to Gate City to the Sheriff.* He finally fell into an exhausted sleep for a little while.

Fortunately, Sam had no idea that Alma and Ezra were on Diamond's back, flying at full gallop in the dark, away from the soldiers, away from civilization and the danger it held for Ezra. Diamond was worked in a lather, but he'd run this way up these old logging trails many times, so Alma knew she didn't have to worry about not being able to see. When Alma and Ezra got to the top of the ridge, Ezra reached around Alma and pulled on the reins. "Let him rest a minute," he said, "and let's change places."

"I can handle this horse, thank you very much." Alma kept on holding the reins as Ezra slid off the horse and grinned up at her. "I know that quite well. But you don't know the way like I do. Watch and learn, girl, watch and learn." He kept grinning at her, and Alma had to smile back. She climbed down off Diamond and handed Ezra the reins.

Ezra took them and stepped in close to her, slipping his arm around the small of her back. He rubbed the dirt off her chin and pulled the old felt hat off her head.

"I've dreamed of this many a time, but you weren't made up like a boy in my mind. That was a crazy brave thing you done, Alma. You saved me. Thank you for doing that."

Alma realized she was holding her breath and inching closer to him. Her heart beat even more wildly now from the fear and the hard ride and from the touch of his hard arm on her back.

"I think about you all the time, Ezra." She couldn't believe she had said it out loud. Her face flushed. She looked up to try to make a joke and cover her embarrassment just at the moment when Ezra started to kiss her, and they bumped noses. "Sorry." "Sorry." He said, "We better get going before those guys come back."

They got mounted up, this time with Alma hanging on behind, and Ezra took off, whirling Diamond down a steep embankment and trotting up a steep gulley. When she realized that Ezra was heading for the creek bluff that was as straight up as Diamond's face, she laid her head against his back and closed her eyes. She knew Diamond could do anything you asked of him, but she also knew that this was going to be scary. She kept her eyes closed until she began to hear the roar of the creek.

The Foam Hole on Copper Creek was one of the most beautiful places on earth. The creek formed a sharp 'S' with an almost solid rock wall forming the backside of the curve and a waterfall pouring down into the pounding foam. The roar from the spring thaw was so loud you had to yell over it to talk to someone. Even Diamond seemed to take it all in, slowing down and looking over at the creek and waterfall. Alma continued to lay her head on Ezra's back, but her eyes were wide open now, and her arms were till wrapped tightly around him, even though there was no danger of falling off on this level ground. The break in the forest canopy over the creek let the moon glow flash off the water and off their skin. Ezra looked down at her tiny wrists, her long beautiful fingers, lying over his belly. The most wonderful thing he could imagine right now would be to be able to just take his shirt off and have her hand touch his bare skin.

"Where are we going?" She said.

Ezra said nothing, only pointed across the creek. *The cave!* She thought. *I'm glad I dressed like a man. I'd never get over there in a skirt.*

Ezra stopped and tied Diamond to a tree that was surrounded on two sides by lots of laurel. He grabbed Alma's hand and plunged into the icy creek. The water was so cold and so swift from the heavy rain and runoff that Alma gasped and stumbled, but Ezra held fast to her hand. The creek was only about 60 feet wide but to Alma, it seemed like a mile. By the time they got across and started up through the rocks to the cave, Alma's teeth were chattering and the wind, which she hadn't noticed before, now felt sharp against her legs. Finally, they came to a little ledge, and Alma thought they were stopping to catch their breath, but then Ezra reached out and moved what Alma thought was a bush growing out of the rock. It was the entrance to the cave.

"Come in." he said. "Ladies first. Watch your head."

They had to bend over at the waist to walk in. About ten feet in, Alma could no longer see anything, and she stopped.

"Go on," Ezra said. "Just a few more steps and you can straighten up. Here we are."

Alma had never been in blackness this deep. Ezra took her by the shoulders and pushed her forward a few steps. Then she felt him bend down beside her. He struck a match and lit a little lantern. The rock walls came alive then and Alma looked around in amazement. She felt like she had stepped into the pages of her World History book from school. All around the cave, Ezra had written and drawn pictures on the walls. It looked like those rock paintings from Egypt Mrs. Barker had talked about.

"Here, put these on." Ezra pulled a pair of pants and a shirt out of a folded quilt and handed them to her.

"No, Ezra, you'll need those. I'll be all right."

"You're littler than me. You're wet almost to your waist. I'm only wet on my legs. We'll let your stuff dry. We need to lay low for a while anyway, Alma. Step right over there and change, and I'll turn my back." He pointed to a little alcove where the light barely reached.

Alma's legs trembled underneath her as she began to pull off the freezing wet clothes. Ezra's pants were so long she was standing on them, and she had to sit down so she could roll them up far enough to walk. When she stood back up, she took off her shirt. She heard Ezra move then and looked around, thinking he had turned to look at her. But he had only taken off his shirt and was standing there with his bare back to her, drying himself with a quilt. He pulled the quilt around him then, like an old woman's shawl, and stood again. Alma quickly put on her shirt and stepped over close behind him.

"You can turn around now." she whispered, almost touching his back. Ezra turned around, opened the quilt and Alma stepped in it, running her hands along his sides. He closed his arms and the quilt around her, wrapping her into his warmth, and they kissed a long and deep kiss, no fumbling this time.

It was too cold and damp, the ground too rocky to lie on, but the couple snuggled together under the quilt, Ezra trembling under the touch of Alma's fingertips on his bare skin. Her kisses were long and sweet, and he could see in the dim lamplight that her cheeks were flushed. Ezra was embarrassed at his appearance, amazed that she would get near him. He could feel her heart thumping as he prayed to keep control.

"Come on, Ezra, to my house, just for a few days. You can sleep in a real bed, get cleaned up. Nobody will know." She held his chin and traced the outline of his lips with her fingertips.

"I will, but not yet. I've got some things I need to do first. I'm going to take you on home."

Alma's face clouded like a summer afternoon. She always expected to get her way.

"Why? What do you have to do?"

"Just you never mind. I've got things to take care of. Once I go in, I'll be in jail or back up at Camp Lee. I need you to do two favors—take my banjo for safekeeping, and go tell Eva I'm all right. Can you do that?"

Before she could answer, he pulled her to him, plunging his hand in the thick tangle of hair, kissing her deep this time, moving his hand around to her throat and across her chest. Alma moaned against his lips, and he let her come up for air. He held her face close to his, and Alma could feel his heart and his quick breaths.

"Sure, sure I will." She whispered.

Ezra pulled her to her feet then and dug another shirt from his dirty knapsack. They picked their way carefully back out of the cave, down over the big rocks to the creek edge. The outlines of the land and sky were emerging. At the water's edge, he turned around and stood with his back to Alma.

"Climb on. I'll carry you back over so you won't get so wet this time." Alma climbed up on a rock, wrapped her arms around Ezra's neck and her legs around his waist. Ezra was so distracted by the feel of her strong legs around him, the sensations of her breasts pressing into his back, that he stumbled a little.

"Hold on tight. I can't hold you 'cause I've got to use my arms for balance."

They plunged into the roar of cold water, Ezra struggling to keep his legs under him as the swift water slammed into them. When they got to the other side, Ezra had to sit down on the ground and catch his breath. He still hadn't recovered all his stamina.

"I've got to go back and get the banjo. You wait."

"No, Ezra, you're weak. Let me do it."

"Now that would be crazy. I just about killed myself packing you over here, and you just turn around and jump in the water anyway." He laughed and shook his head, and then suddenly looked serious. He reached and touched Alma's cheek with the back of his fingers. Then he turned and stepped back into the icy water.

He had an easier, quicker time this time, and in seconds, Ezra disappeared into the cave. He took longer than Alma expected. Alma moved closer to the water's edge. *Isn't he coming back? Did he fool me and slip away again?* At that instant, Ezra stepped back out of the cave with the banjo tied across his back with a leather strap.

When he stepped out of the creek a second time, Alma could feel the cold of the water as she stepped near him. "Here, put this in a safe place somewhere, someplace where it ain't in your way. I ain't sure when I'll need it again." He stopped, a frown on

129

his face, and studied the ground a second. "If anything was to happen to me, you see that Eva gets it, alright?"

He leaned over and kissed her cheek softly. "Thank you, Alma. Thank you again. I'm a very happy man right now." He grinned and wiggled his eyebrows up and down. Alma giggled for the first time that night, and Ezra picked her up and squeezed her until her ribs hurt. "You go on now. I'll be in touch." He let go of her, turned around, and dropped down over the bank without looking back.

"Ezra! Ezra! Where are you going?" Alma was afraid to yell too loud, fearful someone out looking for them might hear her. She stomped her foot furiously and went back to where Diamond was tied.

This is ridiculous! I thought he was going to take me home. She started to point Diamond in the direction Ezra had gone and give him a piece of her mind. Then she remembered what she had promised—take care of the banjo and tell Eva he was alright. Alma sighed and steered Diamond up the steep path toward the old log road.

Ezra hated to just run off on Alma like that; he knew she'd be mad as a hornet. But he would explain it to her later. He hid just down the creek in a tangle of fallen trees and gave her enough time to get up to the first level of the path. He went back to the cave and packed up all his stuff in his knapsack, being very careful to lay out his uniform neatly and roll it up in his blanket so it wouldn't wrinkle.

This was going to be a very tiring trip. It was a long walk over the High Knob anyway, but carrying this much stuff would make it even worse. He left Eva a note in the cave under the Message Rock.

Eva:

Sweet sister, please don't be mad. I'm all right. I'm gone to make some money for us. I've just been walking around like a lightning-struck calf. I don't know why I thought the Army would just slap me on the back and say "Don't worry about it. You go on and have a nice life." I run off from the Army. That's the long and short of it, no matter what my excuse was. They ain't going to take that laying down—they can't. They'll probably lock me up. If I'm lucky, it won't be for long. If I ain't, then that's the way it is. This is my last chance to do something right, something to help you instead of cause you more grief. Please don't worry. I won't be gone long. When I come back, I'll be able to help you out some so you won't have it so hard. Please continue to pray for me, as I will for you.

Your loving brother,

Ezra

Chapter 17

EVA FIGHTS
THE WAR

Because of her father, Eva didn't usually go to church. Once in a while, someone would offer to come stay with him and she'd go, more for the chance to get out and talk to people than to hear the message. But in the winter of 1919, with the flu epidemic still a great fear, Eva was afraid to go anywhere near large groups of people. Preacher Lane or Preacher Cox would come by the house a couple of times a month and visit with her and have prayer. When she looked out the window and saw Preacher Lane on her porch, she opened the door with a smile, but instead of stepping in as he usually did, he backed away from her and stood out in the yard.

"Good morning, Eva. I can't come in. I just stopped by to see if you and your father were all right."

"Well, he's about the same, I guess. You're welcome to come on in." Eva motioned into the house, with a puzzled look on her face.

"No, Eva, I come to make sure you wasn't sick. Everybody, it seems like, has the flu again. They ain't as sick or as many down as before, but the government is closing the schools and county offices anyway telling people to stay home. We've cancelled church until this thing passes. You shouldn't let anybody in the house, Eva, or get near other people. Your daddy wouldn't last three days with this. It's bad."

Eva's heart was pounding as she listened. She knew many were sick, but she'd never heard of the government getting involved in closing churches and telling people to stay home. *Does Ezra know? People give him food. I've got to let him know.*

"If people find out you ain't sick, some of them may be foolish enough to send for you to come help them out or fix them some food, but don't you do it. God forgive me for saying that." The preacher stopped then and turned his hat around and around in his fingers. He looked like he was going to cry, and Eva's eyes filled with tears. "I've got to go pray about it. I know we're called to tend to the sick and all, but after seein' people dying all over..." His voice trailed off. "I never seen nothing like it."

A tear rolled down Eva's cheek and she fought to keep from completely breaking down. More than anything she needed the preacher to stay.

"If I bring you a chair out there, will you sit here with me a while, Preacher? Tell me all about it. I'll bear it." She stepped back into the room and brought a chair out to him. He stepped away from her and let her put it down right in front of the porch step. She went back into the house and stood inside the door.

He named almost every family she knew in the whole community as he listed the homes where the flu had been. This flu hadn't been like times in the past, the preacher said. It didn't just kill the old, the sick, and the babies. It had taken strapping young men and women in the prime of life and in excellent health, often in less than a week's time. Nurses, doctors, and preachers who had gone in to help had sickened and died, too.

"They say it was even worse in the Army. I read in the paper that the Army was losing as many to flu as battle. Audie Vance's boy died the first week he was at Camp Lee. It's a good thing Ezra didn't go back up there after all."

Eva was surprised to hear the preacher mention Ezra. It was the first time ever. Eva knew that he knew about it, of course. But the subject had never come up in their conversations. The preacher would always mention in his prayers with her that her family was going through "difficult times" or a "bad situation," but never any specifics. Eva didn't know if it was because he thought it would embarrass her or because he disapproved of Ezra but didn't want to reveal that to Eva.

"Well, Eva, I've got to go. I hate to leave you after bearing such bad news, but I've got to get around to a lot of other shut-ins and let them know what's going on." He pulled out a pencil and a little book. "Is there anything you need? I'm making a list. It may take me a while, but I'll try to get back around and bring people necessities like flour, meal, salt, and so forth if you don't have enough to do you for the next couple of weeks or so."

"No, that's all right. I'm alright for now. If after two weeks it's still not safe to go to the store, I may need something, Preacher. Thank you so much for coming by."

They had prayer then, the preacher standing out in the yard and Eva behind the screen, heads bowed. Preacher Lane spoke soft and low with a quivering voice, and tears rolled down Eva's cheeks.

He handed her a copy of the weekly Gate City paper and a week-old copy of the *Kingsport Times News*, the only local daily paper, as he almost always did when he came by.

Eva closed the door and collapsed into the chair and sobbed. *Preachers always say the Lord won't put more on you than you can bear, but I don't know about that.* Eva had never known such a desperate time. To add this new plague on top of all the other worries was beyond any stress she had ever experienced. With ten children in the family and a small farm on poor, steep mountain land, life had always been a struggle. But with her father needing care like a baby, her mother and older brothers gone, and now this plague, there weren't enough hands, enough hours in the day.

On top of her anguish over Ezra's situation, there was a shortage of everything. The government had organized a movement to get people to be more conserving with food of all types. They sent teams of town ladies out into the countryside to ask women to sign pledge cards, promising that they will bake no bread and serve no meat at least one day a week. Now, they were saying there was a shortage of cloth because there was no one to pick the cotton, partly, and also because they were using most of it for things the soldiers needed.

What in the world will I do? My quilts were the only thing bringing in any money. I don't know if I'm going to be able to find anyone to help with the canning and getting ready for winter, and I can't leave Daddy here long by himself. Eva pushed the thoughts out of her head and went to walk out to the big tree by the pond. She knew what her mother would tell her to do: pray. Eva snorted at that though. What would Daddy say, if he could? She waited while the pine trees whispered and hissed in the unseasonably warm winds and a cow called to its calf across the field. Then a big grin broke across her face as she remembered the trunk in the storage room.

She raced across the field and ran through her living room, startling her father awake from his rocker by the window. There were old tools and other junk piled on top of the trunk, and it was so heavy that Eva could barely move it a few inches, just enough to get the top to open.

There inside were all kinds of old clothes. Most things were handed down and worn completely to rags from one child to another, but her mother had kept a few things for sentimental reasons. There was a dress made and worn by her great grand-mother. Eva couldn't remember her.

There were aprons brought by the wealthy ladies from Gate City one year. Eva could still remember them standing in their fine clothes on the front porch a few weeks before Christmas explaining to mother that this was their group's Christmas project and how they hoped that the family would have a blessing this holiday. Eva's mother had said nothing but "Thank you kindly" and shut the door. She had then put the aprons in the trunk and never worn them. Until the day she died, Eva's mother had worn one of the same two aprons every day for as long as anyone could remember.

At the bottom of the trunk were the two little gowns and the baby quilt. Eva pressed them to her face and smelled them, rubbing them against her cheek. She was surprised to realize in a few minutes that they were damp from tears spilling silently down her face. She put them back neatly, took the aprons out, and closed the trunk.

Miss Slemp had bought her first quilt called Robbing Peter to Pay Paul. Eva had made one once before when she didn't know what else to do, another time in her life that she had quilted for her very life. She loved the name and the quilt. *That's sort of what I'm doing,* she thought, *giving up memories for money.* She spent the afternoon cutting up the aprons and an old ratty skirt she had patched several times already into little shapes that matched the pattern in the picture. Eva smiled at the thought of what Miss Slemp's reaction would be.

By the time I get this made and ready to take to Big Stone Gap, this flu epidemic will surely be over.

She spent the whole afternoon cutting shapes out of cloth, lost in the work for several minutes at a time. She stopped long enough to feed and change her father and went right back to work. The work so absorbed her that she lost track of time and didn't get supper started until late in the afternoon. Then there were still all her outside chores to do. By bedtime, she was so tired she felt a little dizzy, and her legs and hips ached. She tossed and turned for a while and finally just got up and re-lit a lamp. *I'll look over these papers Preacher brought me. Reading will put me to sleep.*

Minutes later, Eva was wide awake after a small item at the bottom of the front page caught her attention. In Wise County, three brothers who were all "slackers," as the paper called them, were cornered by a couple of deputies and some Baldwin Detectives. The brothers refused to surrender, and one of them was shot dead!

Eva's heart felt like it would jump out of her chest for the second time that day. *God help Ezra. They've hired Baldwins to come after them!* Baldwin Detectives were basically just hired thugs; everyone knew they had often been hired in the past to quell unrest among the miners and to squash any attempt at union organizing. They were bad news. Eva couldn't believe that with the war long over and some troops even starting to come home that the Army would hire Baldwins and have them out shooting people. It just didn't make any sense.

Sleep was impossible now. Eva had to get word to Ezra immediately. He must be extra careful now that Baldwins were here. And he definitely needed to know about the flu being back. He would have to hunt and kill what he ate, making sure he stayed away from people.

Eva tiptoed into the storage room so as to not wake her father. She opened up an old bureau and pulled out one of Ezra's old shirts and a pair of pants and held them up to her. *A little quilt batting is all I need. Alma Newton ain't the only one who can wear pants and ride.* She sat down, penned the note to Ezra, and laid it with the clothes on a chair in her room. Eva went back to bed then, snuggled down under the quilts, said her prayers and went to sleep almost immediately. She had a plan now, so her mind ceased its worrying and let her rest.

Chapter 18

LOGGING CAMP LIFE

Ezra's plan was to work for a few weeks, making maybe two trips to Knoxville, and have enough money to help Eva out for a while. With such a strong demand for timber, the logging companies were doing well and paying some of the best wages ever. As long as he was able to work the long hours, he could make the best money available to a man in southwest Virginia, and he meant to do just that. Eva would have a pretty good little nest egg to last a while.

He worried as he was walking over there to the High Knob that someone might recognize him that close to home. He had some cousins in Wise County, and he sometimes hunted up there. Besides, they had put those posters up everywhere with his picture, along with three others in the region. But it was a gamble he felt he had to take.

When he got to the camp, he was surprised at how big it was and how many people there were. There were some tents set up where bosses did the paperwork and where the men could get water.

Ezra noticed a group of men in a circle laughing and talking, and his first instinct was to go over and join them. But he thought about it for a second and decided that he needed to be one of the silent ones nobody noticed. He went over to one of the tents where there were men sitting at tables and told them he wanted work. They handed him a paper to sign and he just put an X for his signature and told them his name was John Roberts.

The work was hard, but Ezra enjoyed it just for the talk, the sound of people laughing or whistling a tune. It was a real strain on him pretending to be one of those quiet, shy people.

The second day as he was standing in line for some bread and water for lunch, he noticed a man standing behind him in line just staring at him. Ezra went on through the line and cast a sideways glance at the man, hoping that he was gone or paying attention to something else. He was still staring at Ezra. After the man got through the line, he brought his food and sat down right next to Ezra. He took a few bites off the bread and a sip of water, and then he stuck his hand out toward Ezra. "The name's Eliot Gibson."

Ezra wiped his hand on his pants and shook hands with the man. "John Roberts. Glad to know you." He tried to sound as casual as he could and didn't look up at the man.

"I believe I know you from somewhere." Eliot Gibson said. "I just can't put my finger on it."

"Don't recall ever seeing you." Ezra said, staying hunched over his food.

"I believe I've seen your picture somewhere." Gibson wiped his mouth on his sleeve. "I believe it was on a tree over on Wildcat Road."

Ezra stopped chewing and froze. He didn't know whether to just deny it, to get up and walk away, leave the camp and never look back, to say that was a brother or cousin on the picture.

"I'm pretty sure it said something on that picture about $50. Yessir, the Lord sent you my way 'cause he knows I'm needing money on account of my little girl that's sick."

Ezra still kept his eyes lowered. "I'm really sorry about your girl, but I'm begging you not to say anything. You don't understand what that would mean. I got family, too." Ezra finally looked into Eliot Gibson's eyes then and didn't look away.

"Well, I don't mean no harm to anybody. I just want that $50 that the Lord has seen fit to send my way. Long as I get the money coming to me, I got no beef with you or anybody else."

"So you'll keep quiet if I was to get you the $50?" Ezra whispered. "Where am I going to get money like that? I don't have $5 to my name."

"They'll pay you good money if you're willing to ride them logs down to Knoxville. Of course, I'll be going with you to make sure our deal is fair and square." Eliot Gibson smiled a little and nodded at Ezra.

"It's settled then." Ezra suddenly felt full and handed Gibson the rest of his bread.

For the rest of that day, Ezra didn't have to pretend he was quiet and sullen. He was furious and dejected at this turn of events. It would now take him much longer to work out any real amount of money to help Eva. She would be worried sick, but he knew Eliot Gibson would turn him in if he disappeared long enough to walk back over to Hale Springs to leave her a note about where he was. *I can't do anything right, it seem like. Here again, all I can say is I'm so sorry, little sis,* he thought, as he walked over to the tent to volunteer for the dangerous work of rafting the logs down to Knoxville.

EZRA'S JOURNAL

<u>Spring 1920</u>

Walking over the High Knob has give me a lot of time to think, more than I really wanted. I can't get my mind around all that's happened. Having them Army men get me like that after all I done and everybody helping me and then I just get caught like a dumb rabbit in a trap. And then those Home Guard fellows showing up. Was that just an accident or was they following the Army fellows?

And I don't know what to say about Alma. I can't get over that girl. It's all just turning over and over, and I can't get my mind quiet at all. Maybe I should just keep walking and never come back. Alma comes from a good family. I wonder what her daddy thinks about me. It's just really hit me hard what I done. Hearing that Army officer call me a coward, thinking about what it would feel like to have to ride into town in handcuffs. It just makes me feel sick to my stomach.

The worst thing of all is them Army men got Father and Son. Them was my grandpa's guns handed down to me, and I let somebody take them away from me. I don't know how much lower I can go.

Log Riding

It took me the better part of two days, but I walked over to Fort Blackmore, down Stony Creek, then up over the mountain to the Wise County side. There's a big logging operation going on over there, and they're dragging logs out to the river and floating them down to a sawmill. I got me a job. I told them my name was John Roberts, and I didn't care to work at anything they needed. The foreman was a skinny little fellow, kind of nervous, and he just grunted and pointed me toward a group of men. They seem like good fellas, and they showed me what to do. Our job was to put chains around the logs so the horses could drag them. It was killing work, but I was tickled to death to be doing it.

When we finally got all those big horses hooked up to a log, they sent us to walk along with the horses because we'd have to unhook the logs and tie them together at the riverbank. The woods were muggy hot. To make things worse, a couple of times the logs would get hung up on a tree root or rock, and we'd have to stop and grunt and groan, push and pull until we got it to move. But it was all worth it. After we finally got down to the river, we got to rope them together and float them down.

Next Day

I woke up this morning to a dew so heavy you could hear it dripping from the trees. The air smelled so good and clean. I slept pretty sound after I finally got to sleep, and I dreamed about Alma. The dream was too sweet to tell about, and it's give me a whole new attitude. I'm not running away. I woke up with them very words in my head. I won't run out on Eva and Daddy and Alma, not now. No use feeling sorry for myself. And I can't run forever. I got in this mess in the first place because I wanted to help my family. I've got to face what's coming.

Logjam

Today was the hardest work I ever experienced. We snaked some logs down off the High Knob into Stony Creek. Where the water makes a sharp right turn out of the Devil's Fork into Stony, I came to understand how the word logjam came to be. The water was coming out of there with such force that it shot some of the logs straight out of the Devil's Fork and onto the bank. The water was throwing those trees around like haystraws, but then me and James and Hagan had to put chains around them and pull and kick with all our might to get those things back into the water and headed in the right direction.

I have to stop now. I just nodded off while I was writing this. I'll tell you all about it later, Book.

Bad News Again

Book, I hate to even tell you this sorry tale. Once again, my best intentions have come to bad. I thought a couple or three weeks work here at this big logging camp would give me some money to take to Eva. Instead I've been recognized by one of the men, and he says if I pay him the $50 reward that's offered for me, he'll keep quiet. If not, he's turning me in and getting the money on account of his sick little girl. He says the Lord sent this good fortune his way. That may be so. I guess the Lord is so aggravated at me that he's just quit me.

So it's going to take me a good while longer to earn that extra $50. I figure I'll be in pretty good shape if I can work two weeks and then make two trips to Knoxville as a rafter.

<u>March 1920</u>

Hello, Book. Have you missed me? I just got back from taking the first logs to Knoxville, and I'm here to tell you that was some trip. I loved it.

We floated along for several days, sometimes hardly talking at all. The only sounds was from the birds and bugs and the little slap of the water against the logs. It was so beautiful. You'd go from thick woods to steep rock banks and then rolling green pasture land. We seen lots of deer and turkey, and several times we saw huge fish jump out of the water, big as my arm from elbow to fingertips. It's so easy to forget everything when you're floating that way. Anybody on a raft would have a hard time believing there was war and sickness and all this trouble and hardship.

We was lucky on the weather every day except two. One day it poured down the rain. Another day it was hot for this time of year, and the sun was so bright that it nearly blinded us. Most days, though, it was cool with clouds, so it was about as nice as it could get. The cool breeze off the water smelled good and made us hungry. They gave us a whole bunch of bacon to take with us, for some reason, and that's about all we lived on. We had a big piece of tin and we'd stop and get kindling along the way. We'd have that bacon sizzling in that skillet and smoke billowing up. A few times we passed people out working in their fields, and they would all stop what they was doing and watch us pass. I guess we were a sight, six men on a big raft of logs, with a fire blazing in the middle. Eliot Gibson was there, too, and he never let me out of his sight when we got to Knoxville. He's really starting to under my skin. I can't wait to get him his money and get shed of him. They give us money to ride back on the train to Norton. Gibson tried to keep right by me as we got on the train, but I shuffled around and made sure I got to sit across the aisle from him. There's no sense at all in somebody being that tormenting. I said I'd pay him, and I will.

May 1920

I leave the logging camp today with regret. I like this work, and I hope to be able to do it again sometime. It's very hard work and dangerous, too, but it's fun and exciting. Riding those logs down that river was the best adventure I ever had. But I have business to tend to now. I paid off that old Eliot Gibson, and I made him shake my hand and swear he would keep quiet. He acted offended that I didn't trust him. Said I had kept my word and now he'd keep his. He wished me luck and went off grinning with that $50. After all the sweat and beating and thrashing my body took over these last few weeks, I'm leaving this here logging camp with a grand total of $30 in my pocket. That sure ain't much, and it sure won't take care of Eva long if they put me in jail or hang me. But I can't hang around here any longer. If Eliot Gibson slips up and tells, I'll be turned in for sure by somebody. Times is too hard to pass up $50.

The old Devil keeps trying to work on me today, saying "How come you have nothing but bad luck? Where's this here big God you been praying to? If God is who he claims he is, then why did he take Momma like he did, why is Daddy in the shape he's in, why'd I have to go in to the Army, why did Eva's baby die, why is there such a thing as war?" God tells us in his Word that this will happen and not to listen to it, but you can't ignore somebody who's whispering in your ear. Just now a crow flew overhead making that "Caw, caw" sound they do, and all I heard was "Why, why?"

Thinking

I got to fight this, what's going on inside me. I've got to get my mind on something good. I just keep going around and around in my head—first I see Mother on her deathbed, then Eva on the porch, pictures of those Army men, German spies. Then I see my funeral or my hanging or me in jail, and my heart starts to pound in my ears.

The day before I come in to Sam Newton, I got so tired of thinking, so I took this piece of chalk I borrowed from over at Midway school and went back to the cave to draw on the inside. I tried to draw a deer and a trout and a turkey, but I don't have the gift like Eva. They looked like something a little shaver might do. But it stopped me thinking about dying—just for a little while. When I got tired and went to sleep then, I dreamed I was being hanged. I never had such a real dream. I could actually feel the heat of the sun, the rope scratching my neck and smell the horse under me.

It's time for this to end one way or another. I'm not wanting to die, that's for sure. But I've had all I can stand. Eva probably has, too. It's not like I'm helping her all that much as it is. If I become some crazy feller living in a cave that everybody laughs at—that would be worse on her than me being dead. All I can do is face what's coming.

Dear God—I thank you for all the years you gave me with my Momma and Daddy and brothers and sisters. I ask that you bless and keep them. Go with me now as I walk down that lonesome valley. Give me the strength for what's to come. Amen.

Chapter 19

NETTLES VENTS

When the deputy at the front desk in Sheriff Carter's office in Gate City heard someone stomping down the halls with his heels hitting the floor like hammers, he jumped to his feet and put his hand on his weapon. It wasn't unusual for family members of someone locked up to show up and blame the sheriff for their loved one's predicament. The door flew open and banged against the wall. It was Lieutenant Nettles.

"Where's the sheriff?" The deputy knew from his tone of voice that this wasn't a friendly courtesy call.

"Gone to eat. He'll be back in a minute."

"Where's the sheriff? I said." The deputy didn't like the sound of his voice or the look he gave him.

Nettles whirled and was gone before the deputy could finish. He figured the sheriff was either at the little diner across the street or at home. He checked the diner first. When the lieutenant walked in all crisp and clean in his uniform covered with patches and buttons, there was a little lull in the conversation, and many looked him up and down. A few nodded a greeting, but most just bent back to their plates. Nettles spotted the sheriff over in the corner with two other men and went over to him.

"Sheriff, could I have a word with you?"

"Well, since it's obvious I'm eating lunch and it's obvious that you ain't going to wait until I get done, go ahead." He motioned for Nettles to pull up a chair.

"What your problem, soldier?" Sheriff Carter didn't even look at Nettles but blew across his coffee and looked out of the corner of his eye at the man to his right.

"We caught that Teague fellow last night and had him handcuffed and on the way here to the jail. A bunch of hoodlums showed up and held us at gunpoint and let him go."

"Is that so? Who was these hoodlums?"

"How should I know?" Nettles snapped. "That's what I come to ask you. These people are aiding a criminal and interfering with a criminal proceeding of the United States Army. They need to be arrested."

"Is that so?" the sheriff still hadn't looked Nettles in the eye, and his two companions were looking at their plates. Nettles thought he saw one of them smirk but he wasn't sure.

"Is that so? Is that all you can say?

"Look, Lieutenant, I'd like to help you out. But I wouldn't have no way of knowing who that might have been. The Teagues are kin to everybody in the county practically, and them that ain't kin to them still feel sorry for him. So I'd have to go question the whole damn county to find out who that might have been."

Nettles stood up and shoved his chair under the table with a clatter. Many stopped and looked around, and for the first time the Sheriff looked up straight and steady at Nettles. They stared at each other for a minute.

"Or maybe you don't want to question anyone because you don't need to. You not only know who it was, but you were in on it. You bunch of rednecks all stick together, you're—"

The sheriff stood up not two inches from Nettles' face then, and this time everyone stopped what they were doing and stared.

"I don't like your tone, your words, or you, Lieutenant. You start throwing accusations at me, you better have something to back them up, or else shut up and crawl back to wherever you came from."

Nettles knew nothing could be gained at this point and that coming to blows with the local Sheriff wasn't what his commander had in mind when he told him to "lay low."

Nettles turned and marched out of the diner, his back stiff as a poker. He went over to his room at the Compton Hotel and took off his uniform, spreading it neatly on the floor in front of the fireplace, and stretched out across his bed. *I'll give it one more try. I'm not going back to Fort Lee without news of Teague's capture.* He decided not to mention the little escapade last night to his superiors.

After supper, when the cool shade of the mountains began to bring the temperature down, Nettles smoked his pipe and turned in early. Tomorrow he would go see the only person who could help him now.

Chapter 20

NETTLES AND MAC

When Nettles awoke the next morning in his room at the Compton Inn, he felt as stiff and sore as could be, reminding him of those first weeks so long ago in boot camp. He was so tired that his arms and legs felt heavy. His inability to catch even one of these outlaws was turning this whole thing into a career issue, not to mention a blow to his pride. *When I started this, I thought I'd be done with this in a couple of weeks. I really didn't count on anything like this. It's funny how life sometimes has other plans.*

He swung his feet over the edge of the bed and looked down at them. They were knobby and calloused. His toenails were long and ragged. He felt his scratchy face and looked toward his razor and the washbowl. He stood up slowly and grimaced, as he shuffled over to the little mirror on the washstand. Nettles shook his head at the reflection staring back. *I look like my dad. I'd never really noticed it before.* His dad would have known what to do. He had personality, as the saying goes. Everybody liked Jimmy Nettles.

He connected with everybody. But as a boy, Roberta Nettles had managed to instill an air of patrician politeness and distance in her son, not to mention polish and proper speech. Nettles had done everything he could to not be Jimmy Nettles, to reinvent himself in some new species. It had helped take him far in the Army—the crisp discipline and attention to detail, his quick, decisive style of leadership.

Nettles splashed the water into his face with force, splattering the floor and wall a little, scrubbing hard, trying to wake up his senses. Looking back up in the mirror, he saw he was still Jimmy Nettles' son but without any of his redeeming qualities. He was in trouble here, and he knew it. He had the man in custody and couldn't keep him. The locals didn't like or trust him, and they weren't going to help. Embarrassment, rage, and frustration had taken hold of him in a physical way; his face was flushed, and he felt a little short of breath.

To compound his anxiety, his local guide, Mac, had already begun to project irritation at Nettles and was losing his enthusiasm for helping in any way even before the fiasco last night. Mac had begun to offer many excuses lately on why he was now too busy to help Nettles go look for Ezra and the others. Only after much talking and an offer of more money did he finally agree to take Nettles on up the valley toward Russell County and show him that country. They had been headed that way when they had just accidentally run into Ezra the night before. After all that effort, they had caught him quite by accident; he had just walked right into them.

When they had Teague in handcuffs sitting around the fire, Nettles had noticed Mac talking to the prisoner, giving him food. Nettles noticed, too, that Mac sat over close to him and not with Nettles and his men, as if he wanted to say to Teague, "I am with you, not them." After the locals had stormed into the camp and set Ezra free, Nettles saw a distinct look of relief on Mac's face.

Nettles shaved and dressed slowly, as if he was standing in deep mud. *This won't be easy. If there's any little bit of Jimmy Nettles in me anywhere, I need him to come out now.*

Nettles bought a ham biscuit from the ladies down in the restaurant and headed out of town. The biscuit wanted to stick in his throat, but Nettles made himself finish it. He knew this could be a long day.

When he got to Mac's house he stopped at the front door, straightened his uniform and hair, took in a deep breath and blew it out slowly, and finally knocked. Mac stepped up to the door then with his wife over his shoulder. Nettles tipped his hat to her. "Good morning, ma'am. Sorry to disturb you. Could I have a word with you?" Nettles looked at Mac.

"I'll be back in a minute." Mac said over his shoulder. "Let's step out here, Lieutenant." Mac spit on the ground between them as they stood out in his neatly swept dirt yard. "I've got work to do, Mr. Nettles, like I told you. You ain't gonna catch him anyway, in my opinion."

"One more time," Mac was surprised by the look and the tone. Nettles was almost begging. Mac was embarrassed for him. "I'll up your salary. After last night, this qualifies as hazardous duty anyway."

"You're even less likely to catch him now."

Nettles knew this was only an excuse. Mac didn't want to help him because he now realized how the community felt. They had spoken loud and clear last night. "If we catch him again, Cooper and Smith and I will take him to Gate City, hard and fast, believe me. You won't need to go. Nothing will even be mentioned in my report about you. I need you to help me look in some more of those caves you know about. That's the only thing that makes sense."

Two of Mac's four little children, with bare feet and dirty faces, came peeking around the side of the house at them. Mac glanced up at them, scowled, and simply pointed toward the house. The two boys disappeared like sparks from a campfire.

"Well, I can spend your money as good as anybody's. Those boys need school shoes. Let me get some gear and tell my wife I'm going. But I'm sleeping here in my bed tomorrow night, come hell or high water. What you do is up to you. After this, I'm done."

Mac disappeared into the house, and Nettles walked out under a huge maple tree in the corner of the yard. When Mac came back out of the house and began to get his horse saddled and ready, Nettles got on his horse and waited just outside the gate. As they rode out toward the fork in the dirt road, neither man spoke or looked at the other.

Near Nicklesville, they stopped to let the horses rest and to eat. Nettles had some Army rations with him, and he offered to share. Mac just shook his head and walked off in the woods. Nettles realized after a few minutes that he didn't hear a thing. He stopped eating to listen. The only sound was the music of the trees and birds. He started when a shot rang out. In just a minute, Mac strode back into the camp holding a big rabbit by the back leg. He sat down and began to skin it and cut it into pieces. Nettles marveled at how swiftly he worked.

"My father used to love to hunt." Nettles said, and for a second he thought Mac didn't hear him because he didn't react at all. "My mother didn't like it, though."

"Women is squeamish about it, some of them." Mac said without looking up.

"I bet Ezra Teague is a good hunter, the kind my daddy would've admired." This time, Mac looked up with a hint of surprise. Nettles had never mentioned his family in any way, and he'd certainly never said anything that sounded remotely like a compliment to Ezra Teague.

"Probably so. I do know he's a real good shot with a pistol. I seen him shoot one time at the county fair competition."

Nettles said no more, lost in thought, seeing his father's face, the way he would slap his leg and laugh in the middle of a big story. He had vague memories of being in the woods with his dad when he was very little, but he didn't remember exactly where they were.

All he could remember was the heavy gun barrel wobbling in front of him, pointing at a deer. His father and two of his friends and his uncle Daniel were with him, spread out all through the laurel and other brush watching. His dad's eyes sparkled as he whispered instructions. Young Nettles had squeezed the trigger just like his father had taught him, but to his horror, it only clicked loudly. He hadn't put a bullet in the chamber! The deer, startled by the loud click, took off tearing the brush as he went.

The sad, disappointed eyes of his father, they way the other men barely glanced at each other, the long walk back out of the woods empty-handed—these things Nettles still remembered vividly. *I wonder what Jimmy Nettles would say about Ezra, about me, about the war,* he thought. There would be no way of finding out, of course, since his dad had died two years earlier.

"Hunting, knowing what plants to eat, and so forth—that's why we've not had as much success finding these mountain boys as we have some of the others. If they can keep their food supply up without having to expose themselves to populated areas, they're much harder to find. Some of the others who've tried to do what Teague is doing haven't made it a month." Nettles snapped out of his revelry, finished up his rations, and drained his canteen. "I'm going down to the creek to get more water."

Nettles walked the long way around to get to the creek. He wanted time to think. He was lost in thought, so it startled him when he looked down and realized the soft earth he had just sunk his boots into was a grave. He looked more closely now and realized that what he had first thought were rocks were actually old headstones with only illegible ghosts of words still visible.

Tall hemlocks stood around the graves like dark sentinels. Outside the fence, rabbit tobacco grew tall as his head, and the blackberry tangle was too thick to breach. Nettles turned and moved quickly away from the smothering shroud of trees. There was no air stirring.

The old haul road was pocked with turkey tracks and possum droppings, but it was still smooth enough and flat enough that Nettles could hit his full stride, throwing his long legs out at a quick clip, reaching enough speed to create a breeze. *Today will be the day,* he thought, *we'll catch that little bastard.* At that moment a picture of Eva, sitting there in that chair, reading the Army press release, her little feet turned pigeon-toed under her ragged skirt, came to him. The smooth, perfect skin of her neck, the way her fingers lightly held her hair out of her eyes, flashed in his mind and heart, and he almost stopped walking.

No, I've to finish this and go home and forget this whole miserable thing.

Chapter 21

EVA AND ALMA SCHEME

Eva was sleeping fitfully, dreaming that she was running, being chased by dark shapes, through the woods. The dream was so real she could feel the branches slap her face. Then things suddenly changed, and she was running through the woods again, only this time she was the pursuer, and she could see herself running, glancing back over her shoulder from time to time with a look of terror. She caught herself in the dream and as she fell into her pursuer's arms, Eva realized, looking down at the arms and hands coming out from her and wrapping around herself, that she was Ezra in the dream, seeing the world through his eyes. "Ezra, Ezra, are you all right?" Eva cried and buried her face in his shirt. She woke up then, calling into her pillow.

She made herself sit up and swing her legs over the edge of the bed. It was rare for her to have such a vivid dream anytime, but especially during the day. She hadn't slept much at all that week. It took her a minute to realize that what had wakened her was someone knocking at the door. It was Alma, looking tired and tense.

"Eva, I have to talk to you. Ezra was caught last night, but he escaped. He's all right."

Eva fixed them both some coffee as Alma spun out the whole tale, Eva pressing for every little detail. She had trouble grasping Ezra's good fortune.

"You mean, the Home Guard didn't want to take him in. I figured one of them might want the reward."

Alma shook her head. "I was surprised, too. But they told him to 'get out of here,' and I'm not sure what they meant. If they meant to get away just from the Army guys, or if they meant out of town, out of the county. Daddy says they meant out of here period, because people don't like the Army guys snooping around everywhere. Everybody's nervous enough."

"We need to convince him to turn himself in, Eva. You know I don't want that any more than you do. But it's got to be."

"No!" Eva spoke louder than she meant to, and her father startled and looked around the room wildly. She went over and sat down beside him, patting his knee.

"Haven't you heard about them men being hanged? I saw it in the paper down at the store."

"Daddy says that's different." Alma's eyes burned fiercely. "They didn't surrender. He says the Army sent word out to the papers about making a difference between those caught and those who came in on their own. Killing all of them would make no sense anyway. How are they going to be able to quit hunting for all these men if they ask them to surrender and then hang them?"

"I want him to come in, now more than ever. It's not just these Army folks, and the Baldwins, but I'm worried about this flu, too."

Alma hadn't told her about how awful Ezra looked, how he was so thin his bones looked like they would poke through his cheeks. But she did assure her that the flu wasn't that bad now, that most were recovering and the epidemic seemed to be winding down.

"I have to be get word to him about what all is going on." Eva said. "Will you help me?"

So Alma showed back up at the door the next morning bright and early, as Eva was making herself a pot of coffee. "You must just be living on coffee. You look like something the dog dragged in." Alma said as she came through the door.

"I didn't sleep much last night. I didn't fall asleep until it was already showing light outside. Did you bring some of your daddy's clothes?"

"Right here. Let's get started."

Eva opened the old trunk under the window and started pulling out all of her latest sewing projects, not quilts, but padded vests and underpants that she and Alma could use to disguise their feminine shape.

Eva was getting much better at dressing as a man. She was small and wiry, with a very straight figure. Still, even a slight woman has a curve to her hips that is hard to mistake. Eva had figured this out after getting all her "man garb" on and looking at herself in her mother's old mirror. She pulled a bench in front of the mirror and straddled it. Turning around and surveying the view from that angle in the mirror, Eva could see a shape outlined that she knew any man following her on horseback would notice. *What I've got to do is make myself fatter, put on more clothes so that even when I'm setting down, no bones show.* She tried on different combinations, different layerings, until she was satisfied that, at least from a distance, she looked like a boy or a slight man.

Alma was bigger boned and taller, but she was very curvaceous with a substantial bosom. Eva wrapped bandages around her breasts and flattened them as much as she could. Then she sewed up some quilt batting into a fake belly and padded underpants. When she and Alma finished getting into their garb, they were serious and tense, engrossed in getting ready. Their shared fear and anxiety showed on their faces, stern as judges.

When they were both ready, they each checked one another from head to toe and all around.

"Eva, you're one ugly man," Alma giggled.

"Well, same to you," Eva said straightfaced, and then both erupted into fits of laughter.

"All we need is—" Alma reached into the sack on the floor by the back door and pulled out two cucumbers. She stuck one down the front of her pants, and Eva covered her mouth with her hands.

"Alma Newton, you are awful! No wonder Ezra loves you!" She laughed.

"Does he?" Alma's giggles stopped. "Has he told you that? When?"

"No, he doesn't have to, girl. I just know. ."

"Oh, Eva." Alma ran over and hugged her. "I hope you're right. Now let's go get him out of this mess."

This morning, Eva had gotten everything ready; she had taken care of her father's needs and given him some of the sleeping medicine the doctor had given him and gathered up some supplies to take to Ezra. She was going to talk to Ezra and try to get him to surrender. It was his only chance now.

Eva had the horse saddled and all her supplies ready. She was hoping to get back before her father woke, though it really didn't matter all that much. Even if he did wake up, he wouldn't be aware whether Eva was there or not. Mrs. Elva Peters, her daddy's cousin, would be there, since she came over every Thursday and stayed all day to help out. Eva left her a note saying she had gone to get eggs and had left before Mrs. Peters arrived because it was supposed to rain later in the day. She had a change of clothes with her and some eggs hid in the barn, so that when she got back, Mrs. Peters would have no reason to suspect anything. Eva felt proud of herself as she rode off, sure she had thought of everything and come up with a good plan.

Nettles had started making a trip by the Teague's home almost every day to see what was going on, hoping he might luck up and catch the wandering soldier. He knew that Eva always seems to have plenty of firewood, and once he'd come by after two days had passed and found the tin patched on the chicken house. He knew Eva didn't do that herself.

She's my bait, he thought. *God help me for using this poor woman this way.* After the capture and loss of Ezra on Copper Creek, and his accusation of the Sheriff's involvement with those who freed Teague, Nettles had pretty much taken on the search alone. Mac didn't want to help any more. The commander of Camp Lee sent word to Nettles that he was needed there, but Nettle's pride would have none of that. He sent Smith and Cooper back to the base and asked for some sick leave for himself, using the excuse that his mother was ill and needed him at home for a few days. The commander sent him a telegraph back expressing sympathy and told him he was granted the standard week's leave. Nettles realized this was now way beyond duty's call, but his pride was now more involved than his ambition. *I've got to try one more time. He's spooked now. He'll mess up.*

He rose before down that morning and slipped out of the hotel quietly so as to not wake the other guests. The ride took longer than he anticipated because the fog over Copper Creek was as thick as a bride's veil. As he got closer to the Teague's place, he had to veer off the road and into the woods. He wanted to get around behind the house since he felt sure that was the route that Teague would use. Nettles found a break in the trees on a little knoll to the left of the house. From there he could see both the back and the front of the house.

Although the air was still fairly cool, the exertion of the ride and the dodging of limbs and briars and the weight of his uniform were making him sweat. He had tied his horse quite a way back so any pawing or snorting wouldn't be audible to anyone inside or outside the Teague home. He was wiping his sweaty face with his handkerchief when he heard a sound and looked up. There, coming out of the back of the house, was a man carrying a sack over his shoulder. Nettles froze and held his breath. *I can't see his face, but it's got to be him. Who else would be in there?* Nettles watched, hoping the man would turn around and show his face, but he didn't. He disappeared, leading the horse into the barn. In just a minute, the horse came out with the man up on his back, with the large bundle tied on behind the saddle. The rider turned the horse and took off at a fast trot toward the creek, headed north.

Nettles turned and tried to hurry without making a sound, making his way back to his horse. He turned the horse off the hill and through the pasture fields well out from the house. *If I go galloping through the yard, Eva will see me taking out after Ezra and it will scare her to death.*

By the time he got back to the creek's edge, he was running the horse pretty hard, but he still couldn't see Ezra. *He's going somewhere in a hurry.* Just as Nettles was about to slow down and try to save his and the horse's energy, he caught a split-second glimpse of a horse's tail disappearing into a bend in the path.

As Nettles raced through the woods behind Eva, she kicked her horse, urging him to go faster when they hit cleared land. Eva was scared but exhilarated at the sensation of flying so recklessly, the unusual sensation of cloth on her legs and the heavy boots. Gripping the sides of the saddle with her thighs, she fought to stay on when the horse hit a little rise or soft spot. But Eva wasn't the rider Alma was, and when the horse whirled down a fairly steep gulley in the pasture field, she shot forward and lost her balance, her feet coming out of the stirrups. When the horse bounded out of the gully and started up the terraced rocky pasture, Eva struggled to get one of her feet back into the stirrup.

Nettles was gaining ground as she let the reins go slack while she tried to reach down with one hand and hold the stirrup strap still enough to stabilize her weight again. With one hand off the reins, the horse sensed immediately the lack of urgency. Eva was still reaching down to try to hold the strap, trying to hold on to the reins with one hand and urge the horse on at the same time, when she finally realized for the first time how quickly Nettles was gaining on her.

I can't let him catch me yet! He's close enough to circle back and track Alma when he finds out it's me and not Ezra. Eva looked back at him again and when she did, her weight shifted on the saddle just as her horse turned to the right to go around a tree. As often happens in moments just before a tragedy or intense pain, Eva felt like she was in a dream. She saw her hands moving into the air in front of her, a flash of flank as she passed by the horse's shoulder, the sky off in the horizon, and finally the ground. She had time to even notice that there were a couple of rocks big as lumps of coal that were going to be right under where her legs would land. And then there was just a buzz. Eva couldn't see or hear anything but a high-pitched ringing and then silence.

Nettles was already puzzled and frowning before he saw the rider fall. He was close enough to see the flapping stirrups and the struggle to get them back under foot. *What's the matter with him? Surely he can ride better than that.* When the rider went down and lay motionless, Nettles was irritated at the thought that Teague had gone and hurt himself like a damn fool, and now he'd have to haul him to Gate City to the doctor. He stopped and tied the horse to a little dogwood. The riderless horse went over and stood by Nettle's horse and waited as if he was feeling guilty and knew something was wrong.

Eva was lying on her side motionless with her back to Nettles. He suddenly thought that he was dead and saw Eva's face flash in his mind as she had looked that day sitting and reading the news article he had brought her. He prayed that Teague was alive, for her sake. When he gently peered over at the face to check for breathing, his mouth flew open in astonishment at the sight of Eva there on the ground.

"Miss Teague! Miss Teague!" he spoke loudly in her ear, and she groaned. Nettles gently moved her hands, wrists, and arms, looking for signs of broken bones. "Eva, can you roll over on your back?" She groaned again and rolled partially over. Nettles pressed gently all down her other arm and then began to gently massage down each leg. Nothing seemed broken. Nettles suddenly felt something stir inside him. He wanted to touch her small muscled body again, cradle her in his arms like he did his little nephew who had just been born a few months ago. *I need to keep my mind on my job here,* he scolded himself. Eva opened her eyes and stared at him in an unfocused way.

"Do you think anything's broken?" She shook her head back and forth after an extra second to react.

"Then I'm going to take you home." Nettles tied her horse to his and got her up on his horse in front of him. "Just lean back against my chest. I won't let you fall. You had no business doing such a stunt, Miss Teague. This is what you get."

Eva was too addled to do anything but lay her head back against him. He had taken the man's hat that was not mashed flat and put it in his saddlebags. Her hair was so close to his face that he could smell it, the scent a strange mixture of mint and biscuits, from this morning's breakfast, no doubt, and he breathed it in deep and relished it.

When Nettles and Eva got back to the Teague's, the fog had rolled in and whited out the barn and outbuildings. Nettles could hear a cow chewing nearby but couldn't see it. The only other sound was the soft lowing of a calf looking for its mother.

Nettles helped Eva off the horse and she winced. He tried to carry her but she insisted on moving on her own. He took her arm and put it around his waist, and then he pulled her close to him, letting most of her weight rest on his hip.

Mrs. Peters came to the door when they stepped up on the porch. Her hand flew to her mouth at the sight of him. "Oh, Lord, Eva?" The old woman's face changed from concern to puzzlement and then both at once as she looked at Eva's clothes and boots and the padding she wore under them.

"I'll help her to her bed. She fell off her horse and I found her." Nettles said. He didn't see any sense in upsetting the old woman with the whole story. He hoped actually that she had no idea who he was. The blank look in her eyes as she looked first at him and then back at Eva reassured him that she took him for a stranger.

"Eva, what in the world are you doing, girl?"

Nettles moved her into her bed, and this time the movement brought not only a grimace but a cry of anguish. He noticed for the first time the blood stain spreading on the edge of her pant's hem. "You're bleeding."

"I hit something sharp. I don't know what it was. Mrs. Peters can take care of it."

"We receive first aid training in the military. I have a kit in my pack."

"No, you've done quite enough for one day, thank you." Eva was coming back to herself more fully now. Nettles was her enemy, and this was all his fault. She wanted him to leave. As she was talking, Mrs. Peters lifted up the edge of her pants. There was a deep gash just above her ankle.

"If he's got something to dress that with, you better let him."

Nettles nodded to the old woman. "I'll get the kit."

When he was gone, the old woman looked at Eva, her mouth pursed into a tight pucker. "What in God's name do you think you're doing? Why have you got them clothes on and that padding to make you look fat? If this is something, anything, to do with

Ezra, you better get over such foolishness. He got himself in this mess, and he can get out of it. You better think of your daddy."

Nettles came back in without knocking and spread his kit out on the edge of the bed. Eva saw that he had bandages, tape, and iodine. "If you'll remove the boot and sock, and roll up the cuff a little, I'll clean the wound up." He gestured to the old woman. She obeyed and stepped back out of his way. Just then, Eva's father stirred and began to call out, as he often did, in unintelligible syllables, like a baby in its crib.

"I'll go see to your daddy. Somebody's got to." Mrs. Peters looked hard and disapproving at Eva. "Will you be all right?"

Eva knew she was asking if it was okay to leave her alone with the strange man touching her leg. "Yes, I'm fine. I'm feeling much better. You go on."

Nettles soaked a cloth with the iodine. "This will hurt. I'm really sorry, but it'll clean it up." When he touched the jagged wound, it felt like the time Ezekiel, her oldest brother, had touched her with the poker after stirring the fire. She closed her eyes and gritted her teeth, but some tears spilled out of her eyes anyway.

"I'm, I'm sorry." Nettles stammered, suddenly shy and backward, all the pompous and formal manner gone, and the Big Stone Gap accent coming back into his voice, all in the face of a woman's tears.

"I know you don't mean to." Eva looked at him steadily. "But it still hurts." Nettles said nothing, knowing that her words referred not just to the iodine but to this whole situation. He pressed several layers of clean gauze bandages around and around her ankle and tied them up. When he finished, Eva sat up and examined the bandage. "It feels better." She knew she ought to thank him and part of her wanted to, but the other part wouldn't let her.

"Miss Teague." He stopped and looked back toward the front room where Mrs. Peters was tending to Eva's father. Nettles stepped around the side of the bed, and to Eva's astonishment, knelt down beside the bed and leaned his face in close to hers. "Miss Teague, please don't do this anymore. You're going to get hurt or in trouble with the law yourself. You don't want to give your family more worries."

Eva knew that this was true, but she didn't intend to agree with him.

"He needs to surrender on his own. Like I told you before, it's the only way. The war's long over. The country needs these men. They won't hang him."

Nettles stopped and listened again. He could hear Mrs. Peters talking to Eva's father for now, but he knew she would be back in any minute to check on Eva.

"Listen, I'm going back to Camp Lee tomorrow. They won't give me any more leave to do this. But they'll send the Baldwins after him. Please, Eva, talk him into it."

Eva heard something in his voice that she had never heard before, something in the way he said her name. Eva had loved and married before, and she had known a moment before in her life when she heard a man say her name in such a way that she knew he cared for her. "I'll try." she whispered, though she hadn't meant to.

Nettles patted her head and then looked down at it, letting his fingers just linger a second. "I'm leaving tomorrow going back. You can come and watch me get on the train if you feel like it, so you'll know that I'm telling you the truth. You tell Ezra that I'm gone and he needs to come in now."

Nettles began putting his kit back together as Mrs. Peters came back into the room and inspected the bandage. "Looks good. Does it feel better?" Eva nodded.

Nettles turned to go.

Mrs. Peters tried to smile a little for the first time. "I thank you for bringing her home. Now what's your name again, soldier?"

"Andrew, m'am, from Big Stone Gap. I'm just over here visiting some friends before I head back to Camp Lee tomorrow." He tipped his hat and was out the door before he could get any more questions.

Meanwhile, Alma's trip over to the cave was uneventful. She stopped and hid several places on her way, once in a thicket and once behind some rocks, waiting and listening to see if anyone was following her. Convinced she was alone, she finally went on to the cave and to the Message Rock where Eva had instructed her to leave the note.

Even before Alma stepped into the cave, she sensed something was changed. She crept into the cave and felt to the left of the low tunnel opening for the lantern. It wasn't there. Alma took out a match then and scratched it on the rock wall. It wasn't much light, but it was enough to see that the cave was empty. No clothes or lantern or Bible. But there under the Message Rock was a note from Ezra to Eva. Alma inched her way back out into the light so she could read it. He was telling her that he was going off to work for a while to earn money and lay low, and he would be back.

Alma folded the note and put it in her shirt pocket. She sat down on the rocks and put her head in her hands. He hadn't said where he was going or when he'd be back. It could be a week or it could be a year. Alma felt so tired and heavy that she just wanted to lay down in the cave and sleep. But Eva needed to know about the note, and Alma had washing to do. Her daddy would be mad if he came home to find no clean shirt.

Samuel Newton could tell by the way Alma was holding the reins, letting Diamond plod along like a workhorse that something was wrong. He stepped off the porch and followed her into the barn. "Hey, punkin."

Alma didn't even turn around. She took the bundle off the back of the horse and began lifting the bit out of his mouth. "I'm sorry I don't have any lunch ready. I've had a rough morning."

"Where'd you go?" Sam was concerned by the flatness of her voice. It sounded like something had just wrung all the life out of her.

"I went to look for Ezra. He's gone. He left a note at the cave for Eva saying he's going off to work somewhere for money."

"Did you take it to her?"

"Yes, and she's had a bad day, too. She hurt herself. She fell off her horse this morning and cut her leg." Alma didn't mention the disguises, their plan to distract the pursuers, or Nettles bringing Eva home.

"You need to just keep your nose out of this now, Alma. Let Ezra take care of himself."

Alma threw the currycomb down and walked toward the door. She wasn't in the mood for one of his lectures right now.

"I'm grown, Daddy. I'm grown. I love you, but you have to let me go."

She started to leave, but suddenly all in one flash, she felt an ache in her chest and saw all the long years alone since her mother died, saw him going off into the barn to cry, saw how afraid he was that, for the second time in his life, the woman in his life was leaving him. She walked over and took his hand in hers and brought it up to her cheek. "I'll always be yours, Daddy, but I'm a woman. I'm ready."

Chapter 22

EVA TRIES TO HOLD ON

It took two weeks after the fall for Eva's leg to heal. It was red and swollen with infection, and she winced in pain and hobbled around biting her lip as she took care of her father and fretted over Ezra. She cut strips of cloth and rewrapped it at least twice a day, pouring a little moonshine over it that Ezra had brought her for a disinfectant.

Angry at Ezra, she fumed about his going off like that, after all she went through to try to get word to him. *How could he? What if something was to happen to Daddy?* The logging camp wasn't a safe place to be because of the work itself and because of there being so many people there. Ezra was taking a very big risk and for what? To try to get her a little money?

Her fury and frustration sat in the pit of her stomach like a stone. It made her impatient and tired. She slammed the door of the pie safe a little too hard, forced the knife through the cabbage into the wood of the table, banged the dishes she was washing so loudly in the pan that her father woke up and looked at her.

As the weeks dragged on with no word, something began to happen. Eva just didn't feel like herself. She paced. She slept during the day. She opened her mother's old trunk and looked through it—something that usually made her feel peaceful and comforted and less alone. But now it only made her cry. She got out the last few scraps of paper she had left and began to draw, sketching little scenes from childhood of her schoolmates and teachers. Never one who had a way with words—that was Ezra's and her older sister Emma's talent—Eva had never been one of those girls who wrote in a diary or wrote imaginary love letters. But for some reason, a dam broke inside, and Eva really wanted to be able to pour out the words of her heart. Months of so much silence had turned them into burdens she needed to lay down.

So she turned the drawing over and began to write. First, she penned a letter to Ezra, blasting him for taking off on such a foolhardy mission. Next, she wrote to her mother, reminiscing about childhood, asking her for advice. Out of paper, she searched through her mother's recipes and found some partial pages she could tear off and use. To her amazement, she wrote "To Mr. Nettles" at the top of one page. Her pen continued to move, as if some other hand was guiding it.

I want to tell you that I thank you for bringing me home and doctoring my leg when I got hurt. I've been mad at you, thinking that I wouldn't have been hurt in the first place if it wasn't for you, so that's just another problem you've caused. But I thought that I'm not being completely fair here. You're just doing what you have to do, as I am.

I also think I'm not feeling hard against you because of something I saw that day. It was a different person with different eyes and a different heart who bent down on one knee by my bed and whispered to me in a voice so gentle. I saw something different from what I expected in you, Andrew Nettles. I saw a good man in there, a real good man.

Eva started and looked up. Her mind was flooded with thoughts of his smell, his warmth, the big hand with rough knuckles lying on top of the quilt just inches from her arm. She recognized the feeling and was alarmed by it. *I'm turning into one of those pathetic widow ladies, daydreaming over every man who happens by*, she thought. She wadded up every one of the papers and took them out in the backyard trash pile and burned them watching the little sparks go up, each word creating a little firefly of thought that drifted up and disappeared on the gentle breeze.

Chapter 23

EZRA SPENDS THE NIGHT

Alma sat on the piano bench, her back straight as a hoe handle, her fingertips lightly resting on the keys. She had to do something. She had paced back and forth, back and forth, all morning until the pattern in the braided rug in front of the door was making her head swim. *What if he doesn't come?* She couldn't bear to think of it. Alma had found the note under Diamond's saddle blanket. It read:

"Dear Alma,
I write this note to tell you some things. First, I want to thank you for asking for prayer for me at church. It means a lot to me. Second, coming out there and getting me out of the creek beat anything I've ever seen a woman do, and I'm proud of you. You ought not to have done it, but somebody else besides me needs

to fuss at you about it. Next, I want to tell you I'm coming in and putting myself in God's hands and your daddy's. I'll see you tomorrow."

He said he would come today, and Ezra always keeps his word, she thought. When they were in elementary school, he once told her he'd bring her some mistletoe for Christmas. Even though he got sick and didn't come to school for a week, when he finally did show up, weak-eyed as a sick kitten, Alma had found a sack full of the branches, thick with red berries, under her desk. Another time, Amos Cowan called Eva a bad name, and Ezra promised him "a whuppin'" right after school. Ezra kept that promise, too, and Alma smiled at the memory of Amos' black eye.

A noise outside caused Alma to jump up and run to the door. It was only her father getting up to empty his pipe. Alma returned to the piano and started trying to play her favorite piece, "Für Elise" Mrs. Moorehouse had worked on it for months with her, and it still gave Alma great satisfaction to listen to its rolling melody and realize that her fingers were creating it. But today the notes wouldn't come out right. Her fingers tripped over each other like boys at a school dance. She started over twice. *Where could Ezra be? He was late. He said he'd be here this morning, but it's almost noon.* Alma missed the notes again, and this time she cried out in disgust and slammed her hands hard on the keys.

Alma became so distracted with trying to actually play the piece through without mistakes that at first she didn't even hear the sound of voices on the front porch. When she did finally make out the mumble of two voices, she jumped up and flew through the screen door. Sam and Ezra were standing awkwardly, saying nothing after exchanging a greeting. Ezra was mostly looking at his shoes, and Alma knew he was nervous and embarrassed. Ezra had rinsed off in the creek and then washed his clothes as best he could. With only water and no soap, the process wasn't very effective. And now he was in bad shape, the uniform giving off a pungent odor.

"You can't go into town looking like that. I'll fix you a bath and you can borrow some of daddy's clothes for tonight. I'll clean up your uniform. He's got a razor you can use, too."

Alma smiled at him and then whirled out the back door, the swish of her skirts filling the air with lavender as always. Ezra felt so self-conscious all of a sudden. He started to sit down but then thought better of it and just stood with his hands in his pockets, nervously feeling of his long, scraggly beard and greasy hair. *Lord help,* he thought. *I bet I look like old crazy Uncle Pete, the one all the school girls was so afraid of.* Sam just sat back down in the swing and took another draw off his pipe.

"Come on up here and sit down, Ezra. Whatever she says, we better mind her."

Sam almost grinned as he said it, and Ezra couldn't keep the smile hidden.

"Yessir, I reckon we better."

When Alma came back to the door and beckoned to Ezra to come in, he obeyed while Sam got up and headed toward the barn.

"What I don't know won't hurt me." he thought. *"She's grown. I can't babysit her no more."*

Sam could still remember her words to him that day in the barn. "I'm a woman," she had said. It still didn't seem possible to him, but he knew that, of course, she was and had been a long time. He saddled up his horse and rode out across the pasture to visit his brother Malcolm. Leaving Ezra and Alma there alone made his stomach feel tight, but he was determined, feeling his wife's presence and hearing her voice in his head. "She loves him, Sam," the voice said, "and that's just how it's going to be."

It took almost two hours to get the bath over and the haircut and shave. Ezra sat and smiled in the tub of warm water until it began to turn cold and the skin on his hand and feet looked swollen and puckered. Alma sat in the next room and talked to him through the open door. Separately, both Ezra and Alma wondered where Sam went and when he would be back, but neither of them spoke of it.

As Ezra was drying off, Alma spread quilts on top of quilts in the corner of the front room and told Ezra to try it out. Feeling very self-conscious in the borrowed clothes, he stepped out in the room and looked at the little pallet on the floor. He crawled into the sweet smelling cocoon and pulled the quilts up to his neck.

"How does that feel?" Alma knelt down at his feet and tucked and smoothed the top quilt.

"Wonderful." Ezra closed his eyes, fighting the fatigue that was so heavy it felt like he was going to break through the floor. He slept for about an hour that went by in a flash, just like the sleep of a child, and woke suddenly, his heart pounding, not knowing where he was.

For a few minutes he thought he was dreaming. Alma was sitting in a rocker by the fire in her white nightdress, her head tilted back, eyes closed, her hair down. He couldn't believe it. At that moment, his staring woke her, and she looked at him. They smiled at each other.

In the next room, Sam suddenly opened his eyes from a sound sleep, too. *Something's going on*, he thought, *I better go see.* He got up and began putting on his pants, and then he heard a soft mumble. Ezra and Alma were talking in the living room. Sam held his breath to try to hear what they were saying. Then it was quiet again.

He had slipped in through the back door very late and had seen them both there in the front room asleep. He had tiptoed by the door, seeing Ezra there sprawled on his back in the floor, shirtless, and Alma asleep in the rocker in that white gown, like Sleeping Beauty. She was so beautiful she brought tears to his eyes. *Maybe I should go in there, maybe this is all a big mistake, maybe that voice I hear in my head is the Devil.* Sam continued to listen, holding his breath, waiting for some sign to come as to what he should do. But finally he had gone on to bed, resigned to whatever was next.

Alma rose from the rocking chair then and padded across the floor in her bare feet. Ezra didn't raise his head up off the pillow as he watched her move soundlessly toward him. When she knelt down beside him, he rose up on one arm and started to say something, his heart pounding so wildly that he had a sudden memory of a baby rabbit he'd caught days earlier, how its warm, soft, pulsing body thudded in his hand. Alma put a finger to his lips and then all four fingers, rubbing his moustache and tracing the outline of his lips. He thought *I can't stand this, I can't. But I can't put my hands on her.*

In the next room, Sam stood frozen, with his pants in his hand, and then smiled and shook his head at the picture. *She's got a mind of her own. If I go running in there, she'll be mad as the Devil.* So he crawled back into bed, turned on his side, and burrowed down in the covers. "You can't tell her who to love, Sam". He heard his wife's voice say, and he knew she was right. She was always right. Every time he heard her voice like that, he'd learned that he should listen. After all, it's only natural that she would still be watching out for them. So he pulled the covers up to his ear and went back to sleep.

In the next room, Alma was kissing Ezra with her hand lying gently on his bare neck. *That's it. I've got to kiss her back, even if I get in trouble for it.* He sat up and wrapped his arms around her, pulling her into his cradling arms like a baby.

"If Sam Newton walks in here and catches me, he'll kick my ass four ways from Sunday," Ezra whispered.

Alma grinned and shook her head. She put a hand on each side of his face and pulled him into a long, deep kiss. They held and kissed each other for a long time. No more words passed between them. When the heat between them suddenly rose, they looked at each other, no smiles now, the ache of desire plain on their faces. Alma rose then and went to her room and shut the door. Ezra tossed and turned fitfully the rest of the night, and when he awoke about daylight, the covers were in all directions, and he was lying sideways with his head under the window and his feet out on the braided rug.

Ezra startled and woke up. Alma was grinning down at him. "Get up, Sleeping Beauty." She was wearing pants and the old hat she'd worn the night she saved him from the Army men. "C'mon. It's time to ride."

Ezra got dressed and followed her out, being quiet, as she instructed. He had to hurry to catch up with her as she set Diamond in a swift trot and then a full run out across the pasture, like something was chasing her. Ezra was impressed at her stamina and her bravery, as always, but there was something new now: concern. *She's liable to fall off of there and get hurt bad.* Ezra struggled to pull along side of her. She looked over laughing, and then serious and irritated when she saw Ezra reaching toward her reins.

"Slow down, Alma. Slow down, damn it!"

"What's the matter?" She slowed Diamond to a trot. "Have you forgot that I can ride better than you, or just about any man around here, Ezra Teague?" She had that stubborn face on, and Ezra decided right then that he was going to have to learn to get around that face. *You have to handle a really spirited woman the right way, just like a spirited horse. You want to control them without breaking them.*

"I was just wanting you to slow down so I could talk to you," Ezra raised up in the saddle a little and rubbed the back of his thigh.

"Oh, I forgot. I'm sorry. You haven't ridden much lately. I guess that saddle is a little hard. I'll slow down." Alma nudged Diamond gently this time, and they rode all the way through the pasture to the creek side by side. They tied the horses to saplings and walked down to the water's edge. They crouched down together watching the little minnows, the same way they had done it since they were very small. Alma noticed that Ezra was staring at her and grinning.

"What?" she said.

"Come on." He grabbed her hand and dragged her behind him, pulling her into a little opening between two big rhododendrons. "We need to stay out of sight." He pulled her close.

"Oh, really?" Alma giggled as he kissed her neck. "Is that what we're doing?"

"Listen, Alma. I need to say something to you." Ezra suddenly looked dark and serious, holding her by the shoulders.

"No, just kiss me." Alma tried to pull him to her again, but he was firm.

"Listen, I don't know what's going to happen. I need to tell you something. I don't know what your daddy thinks about all this, about me. I do know what I think about you." He stopped, suddenly feeling unsure of himself, unsure of whether or not this was the right thing to do. He let go of Alma and stood up, looking out over the creek, a sudden lump in his throat. "You've meant a lot to me and my family. You're a very special lady."

Alma stood up and wrapped her arms around him from behind. "Everything's going to be all right, Ezra. And my daddy likes you just fine. He'll like whoever I like."

When Sam Newton woke up, it wasn't daylight yet. He quickly shaved, washed his face, and put on a clean shirt. He was out saddling up the horse to go looking for them again when he caught sight of them coming out of the clearing to the west. They were leading Diamond and old Glory, walking along side by side. Alma had that ridiculous hat off and her hair was down. They both looked happy and relaxed.

Sam watched intently, holding his breath, as if that would allow him to hear them all the way back here. Ezra reached out and touched Alma's hair, saying something. They climbed through the fence and walked side by side, not touching, not talking, but close, and Sam thought they looked like an old, long-married couple. Sam shook his head and smiled at that thought, despite a twinge in his chest. If he could have his way, Alma wouldn't be involved in any of this in any way. But a man can't control everything, certainly not the heart of a woman.

He turned and went back into the house, into his room, and shut the door. He heard them come in talking quietly. Alma laughed a soft, sweet laugh that Sam had missed so much, three times in just a few minutes, and Sam closed his eyes and pretended it was Sarah in the next room. He had rarely heard that laugh lately, and he cherished the sound, letting it settle right into his heart. *I'll leave them alone. Maybe Ezra can make her laugh some more.*

Sam drifted off into a twilight sleep for a little while; then he woke to hear light noises coming from the kitchen and began to smell the faint smell of wood smoke from the stove.

When Alma called Ezra to the table, there was a steaming platter of country ham and eggs, gravy, hot coffee steaming from the cup. She had set the table with pretty dishes and a flower in a vase. Sam was filling his plate.

"Well, sit down. Don't just stand there looking at it until it's cold," Sam said.

"You really don't have to go to all this trouble just for me. I really ain't that hungry," Ezra said.

"She didn't do this for you. She fixes me this stuff every morning, don't you, girl?" Sam looked kind of irritated.

"Oh, right." Alma nodded, but when Sam looked away to reach for the gravy bowl, she rolled her eyes and frowned at Ezra. He dropped his head and began eating so Sam wouldn't see him grin.

"I'm going into town to talk to some people this morning for you." Sam spoke after several long minutes of silence.

"I really appreciate that, Mr. Newton," Ezra said.

Sam looked at Alma and sighed. "You're welcome," he said to her.

Sam went out and started getting the horses saddled. In a little while, Ezra came through the gate, tugging at his uniform, Alma right behind him, and across the yard with his hand outstretched. Sam looked at him for a moment, and then took it. "Are you ready?" he said. "I am," Ezra said, "and I'm grateful for your help, Mr. Newton. I owe you."

When they got into town, it was as if someone had sent a telegraph to everyone that he was coming in. Ezra felt very uneasy as everyone stopped in their tracks, it seemed, and he saw some begin to point and talk. Those wanted posters had been up everywhere so long that he was the most famous man in Scott County.

Just as they pulled up to the sheriff's office, two little kids came running out, and Alma and Ezra had to rein their horses to a quick halt. A little freckled boy in a hat two sizes too big handed Ezra a piece of licorice, and the little girl with him just reached out shyly and touched Ezra's boot. "Everyone's on your side." Alma said.

Chapter 24

EZRA IN JAIL

Eva got Sally McConnell to come stay with her father so she could go see Ezra in jail. She took him some clean clothes, one of her quilts, some old cornbread and biscuits, and a drawing of her dad as a younger man walking behind a mule plowing the garden. She put on her best dress and pinned her hair up. Her stomach felt queasy, so she only drank a little coffee and ate part of a biscuit. *What will I say? Will he be different?* She wondered as she rode along toward Gate City.

When she got to the jail, Sheriff Carter led her back to Ezra's cell. He seemed almost sad and a little embarrassed to see her.

"Are you all right?" she said, sounding more anxious than she meant to. "Are you gettin' plenty to eat?"

"I'm fine. You're the one needs worryin' over." he said. Eva looked at Sheriff Carter, then down at the basket she was carrying. "Can we give him this now?"

"No, not right now. You leave it with me as you go out, and I'll see to it he gets it." The sheriff stepped back out to his desk, leaving the door open between the cells and the office. Eva gave him time to sit down and back to work.

"Ezra, what have you heard? What's going to happen?" Eva pressed her face to the bars and lowered her voice to a whisper. Ezra reached through the bars and patted her cheek.

"There's gonna be a hearing with the local draft board members and some Army officers from up at Fort Lee. Alma's got Ez Wolfe lined up to stand with me, and she's got everybody from the Preacher Bellamy to Miz Slemp from out Big Stone writing letters on my behalf. She's something."

"Yes, yes, she is. She's a good woman, Ezra." Eva whispered. They stood silent and awkward for a moment. Then they heard the front door open, and a voice Eva thought she recognized said, "Good afternoon, Sheriff. How are you?" Eva turned. Lieutenant Nettles stepped up to the Sheriff's desk with an outstretched hand. He froze as he saw Ezra and Eva through the open door. Nettles removed his hat and nodded. "Good day, Miss Teague."

"She come to bring him some clothes and some extra food." Carter grinned. "You know how these women are." His smile disappeared as he saw Ezra and Nettles stare at each other.

Nettles stepped into the open door of the cell block. "Like I already told your sister, Mr. Teague, this hasn't been personal with me. I had a job to do."

"I know that." Ezra said. "I appreciate how you got my guns away from the fellow out there on the creek that night, but I don't appreciate you going out to my place and threatening my sister."

"He didn't , Ezra." Eva spoke quickly, and Ezra looked surprised. "He didn't threaten me or you, really, that day. I didn't mean to make it sound like that. I was just scared because of you. He's the one who told me about the announcement from the government about going easy on the ones who surrendered. And he picked up Daddy when he fell out of his chair."

Ezra stared at his sister as she looked back at Nettles. Nettles' face flushed and he stammered. "Well, yes, well."

Sheriff Carter stood watching, and his expression changed as he looked at Eva and Nettles. He cleared his throat. "Eva, you're gonna have to come out of there if Lieutenant Nettles want to talk to the prisoner."

"No, sheriff, that's quite alright. My duty in this matter is done except for tomorrow. That's what I came to tell you. The hearing will go forward tomorrow morning. The two officers coming from Fort Lee got on the train up there this morning." Nettles turned back to face Eva and Ezra. "I assure you both that this will be a fair and full inquiry. After all, this is the United States Army." Nettles looked at Eva like he wanted to say something, but he just put his hat back on and left.

The sheriff let Eva stay until Ezra ate his cornbread. She showed him the drawing of their father, and they both teared up a little. Then they hugged each other as best they could through the bars, and Eva left.

Tomorrow is it. The day I been dreading. Ezra thought. He stood up and paced around in his cell a little. The cell was 5 feet by 7 feet, the bed covered with one gray scratchy wool blanket on one side, a slop bucket and a stool on the other. Ezra sat with his head back, like a baby bird waiting for its mother, looking up at the tiny window on the back wall near the ceiling. The chimney flue from the stove in the basement ran up through his room, so there was a short wall that stuck out on one side of the window. Ezra had found that he could put his back against the far wall and use the little wall to "walk" up, pushing himself up high enough to see out the window.

He could see into the yards of the houses across the street from the courthouse and jail. Occasionally one of the little ladies would come out into the yard to feed her cats or tend her flowers, so Ezra stayed up there and watched as long as he could, until his leg muscles would begin to twitch and jerk, and he would fall back down onto his bunk.

Ezra was hanging up there like that later when Alma appeared at the bars. She looked scared and jumped when the deputy barked, "Get down from there right now!" Ezra dropped to the floor, looking a little sheepish, like a kid caught by the teacher.

She came every day to see him, bringing him cornbread or cake, a flower. Nothing got much reaction from him, and Alma could see that he was beginning to wither. She knew he couldn't stand being cooped like this much longer.

"You've got five minutes," the deputy said to Alma, and walked out, slamming the heavy door behind him.

Ezra was not paying any attention to anything at that moment except Alma. Her hair was down, brown silk that tumbled all around her shoulders. She was wearing a beautiful high-necked dress in a style Ezra had never seen before, with a little diamond shape cut out on her chest, revealing the smooth skin and the tiny peak of cleavage. There was one delicate curl of her hair lying right inside the diamond on her almond skin, and Ezra felt that weak feeling in his stomach.

"I need to ask your forgiveness for something." She put her hands around the cell bars and pulled herself close to him.

"Why? What are you talking about?"

"I read your journal. I'd never read the Song of Solomon before. I didn't know there was things in the Bible like that."

"I can teach you a lot of things about the Bible." Ezra brushed his lips across her fingers and then wrapped his hand over hers.

Alma reached into the basket she was carrying. She brought a robin's nest with one perfect blue egg in it.

"I found this on the ground at the house."

Ezra picked up the tiny egg and studied it for a second.

"Have I told you that you get prettier every day?"

Alma smiled for the first time.

"Your shirt smells. I can wash it for you."

Ezra stared at her and unbuttoned his shirt. Alma laid her hand on his chest.

"I don't want you to have to do this. No man oughta have to live filthy like this. Alma, what if I never get outta here?"

Alma reached into her basket and handed him a turkey feather.

"This is to remind you of things that are free. We'll get out of this somehow, I know it."

After Alma left, the sheriff came out of his office. "I just wanted to let you know that the lieutenant gave your guns to Eva and let her take them home. That was good of him. He could have kept them, you know."

Ezra stood up and grinned, and then he remembered the look that had passed between Eva and the soldier and frowned. "Well, that's good. And he ain't the sort of fellow who would steal something, not even from me."

The Sheriff nodded and seemed to be thinking what to say. "He ain't a bad man or anything. He's just doing his job, just like I am, Ezra."

Ezra nodded and went back over and sat down on his bunk. "What do you reckon they'll do with me?"

"I don't know, Ezra. The Army don't seem to have much stomach for hanging the deserters anymore, so you should take comfort in that. But they might put you in the brig up there at Camp Lee. If they do that, I'll do everything I can to get them to let me keep you here where Eva can come see you. And anybody else that has a mind to." The Sheriff grinned and gestured toward the little basket.

"I appreciate that." Ezra said. "I do."

EZRA'S JOURNAL

Dog Days 1920

I don't see why they won't let me have my banjo in here. It ain't like I can use it for a saw and cut my way out of here or threaten the deputy with it. As big a fellow as he is, if I was to hit him with it, it would just bust it into a million pieces. They want you to be miserable, I reckon, and I guess jail should be that way. I was just sitting there thinking about playing music and how much fun it is. If I get put in prison for life for this, that's going to be what hurts the most after being away from my family and shaming them. To think I might never play music again makes me want to cry.

And I just got to thinking that now I might not ever do a lot of things I thought I would, like get married and have younguns, get baptized, and learn to play the fiddle. I have always wanted to play a fiddle most of all. Sometimes I dream I can. In my dream I can make my fingers move on the neck light and quick as a gnat, and the bow is always on the right string, which sure ain't how it goes in real life. I've tried to play one a few times, but it just made me go crosseyed and tense.

It takes something special inside you to play a fiddle. Every fiddle player I ever knowed had a strong spirit somehow. You have to believe in yourself. You got to have nerves of steel. The neck is so much littler than a banjo neck, and there ain't no frets to help you find the notes. If your finger is off by a thumbnail, it will make the note come out sounding like a cat with its tail under the rocking chair.

That's why so many fiddlers play with their eyes closed. Your eyes ain't no help to you. It's got to be in your fingers, they just know where to go, and in your soul, and in your backbone, which has to be tough as a hickory fence post. You have to surrender to it completely, or you'll not be able to do it.

Book, I forgot to tell you some very important news. The lieutenant brought Father and Son back to me. I have to say that was nice of him, and I won't forget it. I think, though, that he had a motive. I didn't much like the way he was looking at Eva, and what's even stranger, she didn't seem to mind it. It's a good thing that all this is about to come to a head, one way or another. I need to try to keep an eye on Eva. She needs watching after. All this has been too hard on her, and I know she gets lonely. I can't say nothing to him now, in the fix I'm in, but I mean to have a word with him at some point about just exactly what he's thinking and what's already went on.

Jailhouse—1920

The smell is really getting to me in here. It ain't natural to make a man sit and smell his own filth like this. I have times when my heart starts to race so that I can't hardly breathe thinking I might have to stay like this for a long time. Sheriff let Alma bring me my writing book and my Bible and a book of poems Mother kept from school. Alma—I like writing her name, like I was in grade school. How did God know to make a woman like her for me? Yesterday when she come, she brought a robin's nest with a sky blue egg still in it, and a perfect stone from the river below the bridge, and a turkey feather, all to remind me of things that are free, she said. So I must have hope. Paul said, "Faith, hope, and love, and the greatest of these is love."

189

Chapter 25

THE TRIAL

Ezra sat staring straight ahead and sweating. He could not look at Alma. His chin was still stinging from where he had cut himself shaving that morning. Alma had cut his hair and bought him some new clothes that fit. Any other time in his life he would have been walking around grinning and bragging on himself, if he could find the right audience, about how good looking he was. "Look good enough to bury, don't I fellers?" But he felt too heavy to even manage a grin today. Everything possible had been done; now it was all over. His time had come.

Ezra was grateful for all that had been done for him. Alma had coordinated a letter-writing campaign from every prominent person she could think of: the current sheriff, some teachers, even his old school superintendent, Mr. Rambo. The letter that had touched him the most was from Preacher Bellamy:

I know Ezra Teague is a child of God. He was simply forced to choose between man's law and God's law, and that's what put him in the predicament he's in now—not cowardice, not lack of patriotism, not willful breaking of the law. I think Mr. Teague has suffered enough for one lifetime.

Ezra jumped as a door flew open at the back of the room and a solemn line of uniformed men made their way to the front tables. Their faces were a blank slate, solemn and clean. The prosecuting officer, a Captain Banks, stood up after the official announcements and instructions to the spectators.

"I intend to prove to the court that Mr. Teague, by remaining AWOL for the time that he did, committed treason. I will prove that he had many opportunities to turn himself in. His selfish decision was to abort his duty to his country and go gallivanting around southwest Virginia for nearly two years at great expense to his country, and that his treasonous act calls for nothing less than imprisonment."

The Captain sat down. Ezra began to tremble a little, and his mind went sort of blank. When his defender, a fellow from Camp Lee named Arwood, stood up to speak, Ezra only caught parts of his statement. In his mind, he saw the water running over the periwinkles at Hale Springs, his banjo leaning against the wall of the cave, imagined the constant wind up on Bear Knob. He closed his eyes for a minute and went here in his mind, wondering if he'd ever see those places for real again.

"I call Private First Class Gyles Cooper to the stand, please."

Why in God's name is he calling that lunatic? Ezra thought. Cooper stood up looking surprised, looked at Nettles who had turned around to stare at him, and then came hesitantly up to the front of the room. He sat down only after Captain Smith told him to, and the panel of officers at the table leaned forward, anxious to get started.

"Mr. Cooper, did you know Mr. Teague at Fort Lee?"

"Yessir, I knew who he was. I seen him shoot a couple of times."

"Was Mr. Teague a willing and capable soldier in your estimation?"

"Sure was. He was one of the toughest fellows we had up there. I hated to have to come down here after him. He made my life a hell for over a year."

"Take a look at this memo, Private, placed in Mr. Teague's folder by Sergeant Major Fred Fielding." Arwood handed a paper to Cooper. The young soldier, lips moving softly, looked closely at it and began to nod. Arwood took the paper and handed it down to the panel. He then read from it to the court.

"Teague is an excellent marksman and very coordinated. He's bested all the new recruits on the firing range and the obstacle course. Consider for special duty."

Cooper grinned a little and nodded. But his face went serious when he caught Nettles frowning at him.

"Can you corroborate that, Private?"

"I don't know what that means, sir."

"Are those statements true about Teague?"

"Oh, yessir, far as I know."

Nettles was the next witness called. He walked very straight and proud up to the stand and read a long prepared statement to the group, detailing every aspect of the mission. The panel of judges listened intently for a while, but Ezra began to notice a couple of them squirming after Nettles had been going for twenty minutes or so. Finally, Nettles concluded with a self-congratulatory note.

"Although we were unable to deliver Mr. Teague to the appropriate authorities ourselves, there is no doubt in my mind that the persistence and diligence shown by my patrol throughout this long search led him to surrender. They are to be commended for their dedication to duty and to country during this difficult time."

Ezra's counsel stood up.

"Lieutenant Nettles, exactly how many times would you say that you or someone under your command actually saw Mr. Teague in Scott County?"

Nettles cleared his throat, stalled for a time by pilfering through his papers for a minute, but finally answered. "Well, I believe three, maybe four times."

"Three times? In almost two years?

"Yes, sir."

"Private Teague stated in his deposition that he never went outside of an approximate 40 mile area in almost two years and you only saw him three times. Wouldn't it be fair to say, Lieutenant Nettles, that you weren't really putting much pressure on Ezra Teague at all? Couldn't he have left the area and escaped at any time without any detection at all?"

Nettles' look darkened as he saw the direction the questions were taking.

"I don't know about that."

Arwood laid his papers down and moved closer to Nettles.

"Isn't it true, Lieutenant, that Mr. Teague's skill and knowledge of the area made your job, for all practical purposes, impossible?"

Nettles hesitated, obviously searching for something to say that would rescue him. The counselor continued.

"Since Mr. Teague could have escaped at any time and never been seen again, why did he stay around?"

"Because of his family, I understand. That's what started the whole problem in the first place." Nettles looks at Ezra for the first time. "They're very close."

Captain Arwood walked over to the table and scribbled something on a piece of paper.

"Lieutenant, can you or anyone in your patrol testify to the fact that Private Teague was out of his uniform?"

The courtroom began to buzz. Ezra tried to swallow, but his mouth was so dry his tongue wouldn't move. Nettles had a stricken look on his face. He rifled through his papers a minute, but then looked up slowly at the Captain.

"No, sir. I don't think so."

"All three times you saw him."

"Yes, sir." Nettles voice was quieter, and he was not staring directly at anyone now.

"No more questions." Ezra's advocate stood and spoke softly to the panel. "I think we've all heard enough."

"Wait." Nettles looked surprised to hear his own voice. He looked down at his hands. He couldn't believe what he was about to do. He knew deep down why he was doing it, but it still made no sense. *After all this,* he thought.

"Mr. Teague got into this trouble because of this family. They're very close. I don't believe he's a coward like most of the other deserters. And he turned himself in. According to the newspapers, that's supposed to mean he gets favorable treatment."

Nettles finally looked up at Ezra, the men at the table, at Eva.

"The U. S. Government must keep its word and not make an example of him. The integrity of our government is more important than some little hillside farmer." The counselor told him he had no further questions, and Nettles got up from the chair and walked out of the room with his eyes straight ahead.

They told Ezra to wait when the group finally finished hearing from the other two cases that were before them. The two men from Duffield that were there had not turned themselves in and had been caught by the sheriff. They didn't seem to have too many supporters in the room, and they knew it. One of them broke down and cried like a schoolboy, and Ezra was embarrassed for him and his family.

While they waited and waited for what seemed like an eternity, Alma sat quietly by him, occasionally squeezing his arm. She didn't seem nervous at all. Ezra would sneak looks at her, not staring too long and making people talk.

The jailer took Ezra and the other men back to the jail to wait for the decision. Alma walked with them, ignoring the stares as she went by. She sat down on a stool outside the cell and held Ezra's hand and patted it every now and then. Ezra was sweating some, but Alma looked as cool, clean, unruffled as when the long day had begun. Ezra smiled and shook his head when she wasn't looking. *She's as cool as a cucumber.* He marveled at her nerves of steel. *I shouldn't be surprised, though. Anybody that's ever seen her ride like a wild Indian on that horse should know that she ain't no sissy.*

Before long, they sent for them to come back to the court. As the door opened and the Army officials filed back into the room, Ezra tried to read their faces and struggled to control his emotions. His heart was pounding so hard he was having trouble breathing.

Things didn't go so well for the other two. Captain Banks read the decision of the group: both of them would go back to the brig at Fort Lee for two years. Ezra swallowed hard, and he could sense Alma stiffening beside him, her face a blank. *Here it comes,* he thought, *but I can't say I don't deserve it.*

"Since Mr. Teague responded to the call to surrender on his own, and since we have no evidence that he left his uniform, and we have a tremendous outpouring of testimonials concerning his character, his case is somewhat different," The Captain told the crowd with a different expression on his face now. "The military and the U. S. government are not indifferent to the difficult decision Mr. Teague found himself in and the expectations his family placed on him. And we have to agree with Lieutenant Nettles that we must keep our word on this issue. So we have decided to award a dishonorable discharge and leave it at that. His time in the woods away from his family and community will suffice as his time served."

Ezra was so surprised he didn't react to the words. As Captain Banks was thanking the local sheriff and members of the draft board who had been involved in "this difficult business," as he called it, Alma was grinning from ear to ear, and she linked her arm through Ezra's and squeezed it to her chest. They stood, Ezra stunned like a man who'd just been punched, as people swarmed around him and slapped him on the back. One of the men from Duffield was crying on a woman's shoulder, and the other stood alone, with no family there at all, evidently, until the deputies came and let him away.

Lieutenant Nettles got up, gathered up his belongings, and started down the courthouse steps. He was just ready to step into the street and head over to the hotel to gather up his things when he heard a voice, "Wait! Lieutenant, wait!"

It was Teague and that beautiful woman coming toward him, and Nettles turned and faced him square and drew himself up. To his surprise, Teague was sticking out his hand.

"I want to thank you for what you did in there. After looking for me and all. I really appreciate it.

Nettles shook his hand, but only briefly. "That's fine. Just doing my job, son." Nettles took out a big cigar, lit it, and started to turn his back on Ezra.

"Can I buy you a drink?" Ezra grinned when he said it.

"You know good and well that's against the law now. Besides, I don't drink."

Ezra waited until he got across the street and then cupped his hand and yelled, "Well, some of these days, you oughta start."

Nettles turned around and grinned back in spite of himself. He checked out of the Compton Hotel and for the first time in two years, headed over to Big Stone Gap for a visit instead of back to Fort Lee.

Chapter 26

DREAM DAYS

After Ezra and Alma walked out of the courthouse arm-in-arm that day, Ezra refused to talk about his time on the run, though people were always bringing it up and asking questions. He would just change the subject. All he had on his mind now was Alma and their upcoming wedding. He thought his life was magic now, too good, too sweet, and that other life had been lived by some unlucky fellow.

Sam Newton deeded them the back 40 acres of his farm with some good timber on it for building a house and barn. Ezra got a job down at Dockery's Sawmill to help them get on their feet quickly, and he set about learning everything he could about the business so he could start one of his own. Ezra was a man on fire, filled with a sense of purpose and hope he had never felt before. When Alma got pregnant just a few months after the wedding, they thought they would burst with happiness. Alma danced around the bedroom in her slip and talked all at once about names, things the baby would need, how her Father would be so thrilled. This time Ezra didn't have to look away, and he laughed at her antics, finally pulling her into the pile of quilts with him.

Her pregnancy was hard, though. Alma stayed sick and actually lost weight rather than gaining it. Ezra worried about her, but Eva kept reassuring him that everything would be alright.

The night his baby girl was born, Ezra got the worst headache he had ever had in his life. The pain was so bad he vomited. He had to lie still in a dark room; he could be no help to anyone. When Eva brought the baby to him to see, he pulled the tiny, wet face to his shirt, and father and daughter spent their first moments crying together. They named her Kate and everyone said she looked exactly like Alma as a baby: the same silky hair, wide beautiful eyes, and the most perfect little mouth. Ezra and Alma would lie with her and watch her sleep, more perfect than they could have ever imagined. Alma would talk about all her big plans: for a new house, more horses, taking Kate to visit relatives. She was so excited and eager to get on with life, but also seemed to have a hard time getting her strength back from the birth. She had dark circles under her eyes that never went away, no matter how much she slept.

Looking back on this time of his life later, Ezra would remark that he could barely remember it, almost like it was a dream instead of something real. He would pull out the one photograph he had of that time, a brief moment of happiness captured by a traveling photographer in front of their new home. Alma sits in a straight-back chair, solemn, confident, striking. She holds a beautiful Star of Bethlehem quilt on her lap, with the baby sitting there. Ezra stands beside her, one hand resting on the chair, the other behind his back. They look content, well-fed, and healthy. In the picture, Ezra's expression is a bit bewildered, but blissful, like a man asleep, blessed by good fortune beyond his comprehension. He kept thinking, *This isn't real, this isn't my life. I live in a cave or in Parson's drafty barn.* Something kept nagging at him sometimes, though, and he realized later that it was a premonition. The world was about to give way under him.

Although his memories of that golden, magical year when his life was perfect would blur and fade as time went on, the unraveling of it all was as vivid as the present. It's so strange the way memory is often nothing more than an image. Ezra would always remember that it all started with the red stain turning pink in the washbowl by Alma's bed. She had been coughing for months.

"It's the weeds," she said, and sent Ezra out with the long-handled mowing scythe to cut them down.

But as the cough got worse, Ezra saw a look in her eyes he tried to avoid whenever he could. One night when he pulled her close, he realized the she was losing weight, her ribs showing through her back like horses in a summer drought.

The first day she ran a high fever, Alma asked for Doc McConnell to come and treat what she insisted was pneumonia. The doctor came in smiling, putting on a fake Irish accent and telling Ezra a joke about two Irishmen trying to bribe their way into heaven by offering St. Peter a jar of moonshine. Ezra smiled weakly and didn't return the Irish brogue as he usually did. By the time Doc McConnell finished examining Alma, his face was dark, too, his mouth set in a straight, tight line.

"I'll have to send this off to the lab to be sure. I hope I'm wrong." He put his hand on Ezra's shoulder and looked a long moment out the window.

"I know," Ezra choked and said no more.

"It's consumption, and it's pretty bad. I'm going to throw everything I've got at it. Don't let her out of bed. Get Miss Barker to come help you."

Doc put his hat on, not looking at Ezra, and walked out with his head down.

Ezra couldn't remember much of the rest of the day. Doc had said something about new drugs, about John Baker recovering fully. Ezra heard the Doc had cried that night when he told his wife about it.

His clearest memory was going into Alma's room and seeing her pale, ghastly face and that spreading pink stain in her wash bowl and a tiny drop of pink at the edge of her mouth. He threw the water out the window, covered her up, and went out to the barn. It was far enough from the house that none could hear him cry. He threw up his breakfast—grits and eggs—in a nasty, grayish white pile in the hay, a second spreading stain in his day.

Sam Newton came by every day to check on her. Ezra could hardly bear to look him in the face. Somehow, this was all Ezra's fault. His bad luck was like a disease. Sam's face was a map of grief, of disbelief. He couldn't fathom how this could be—that he was losing another one.

Ezra noticed that Sam was beginning to lose almost as much weight as Alma. When he came in the house now, he could smell the whiskey from his breath. He would sit in her room and just stare at her. If she opened her eyes, he would go over and pat her hand, but if he tried to speak, emotion would choke off the words. He'd just swallow them and force a smile.

Ezra fixed an extra bed for him and sometimes convinced him to stay over, but Sam wouldn't commit to staying with them, although Ezra repeatedly asked him about it.

"She'd like you near," Ezra said.

"No, no, I won't impose. You've got enough on you. I ... ." his voice trailed off.

"It's no trouble. Really. I'd feel better if ... ." Ezra wanted to cry, to put his arms around the old man who had aged a decade in the last few months.

"I can't, I can't." Sam said. He looked once more toward Alma's room and was out the door. He no longer offered to hold

Kate; he couldn't seem to bring himself to look at her unless he had to.

When Sam didn't show up for a week, Ezra got Eva to stay with Alma, and he rode over there. When he got to the front door and it was standing partly open, he got scared. He walked in cautiously, put his hand up to his face in reaction to the smell, amazed at the clutter and filth in the house.

Ezra stepped back toward Sam's room fearful he'd find him dead. But Sam was just passed out, with empty bottles setting all around the room. When Ezra moved Sam's arm, he groaned and turned over. So Ezra tiptoed out and shut the door. *I can't blame him. I'd do that too if I could, if I didn't have to see to Alma and the baby.* Ezra returned to Alma's bedside, resigned now to the fact that he would go through this mostly alone, with only Eva to help him.

For about two months, every day was an unbearable repetition of the one before. Ezra sat by Alma's bed, first in a straight-back woven chair that his grandpa had made, then in the big rocker that used to belong to his mother.

At first some of the medicine the doctor brought made Alma feel better, and she would sit up and eat a little, play with Katie, and read her a story. Her energy was really short-lived, though, because this little bit of exertion would leave her in a need of a nap. She ran a fever all the time, and her face would shine with little beads of perspiration.

One day he fell asleep in the rocker and when he woke up, she was staring at him so intently, her face so white that he thought she was dead. Ezra leaned up to take her hand, and she jerked it away to cover her mouth as the barking cough started again. She coughed and coughed and coughed, catching bloody phlegm in the handkerchief, struggling to sit up as she lost her breath.

Ezra felt his own chest tightening, and he saw the fear in her eyes. The coughing fit subsided, and she lay still as her breath rattled in and out. Ezra laid his hand on her forehead and smoothed the damp hair from her face.

"You've got to tell me how you want that room built on the back. When you get better, we're finally going to get this place fixed the way you've always wanted it."

"I think Eva and Katie will have to help you." Alma looked at him very levelly. "You know what's going to happen, Ezra. So do I."

Alma reached out her thin arms and pulled his head down on her chest. "Already you knew my soul, my body held no secret from you," she whispered. "You can do it, Ezra Teague, you can do it. My father did it, you can, too."

Ezra wanted to raise up his head and tell her she was wrong, that everything would be alright, but his head weighed a ton, and he began to cry hard into her nightgown as she continued whispering to him and rubbing her fingers through his hair.

"Don't make her take piano lessons. Teach her how to fish and don't make her wear dresses all the time." Her voice trailed off in a hoarse whisper. Those were her last words. She slipped off into a coma, and although Doc McConnell tried some more medicines he had just gotten from Atlanta, she died two days later, just as the morning birds began their chorus outside her window.

Until the end of his life, Ezra would see the blood in the water and the vomit in the hay as clearly in his mind as the moment it happened. In his nightmares for years afterwards, he had a recurring dream of Alma covered with blood, vomiting massive amounts, the slime covering her bed, the floor, creeping toward him like a lava flow as he stood in the bedroom door. A few times Ezra woke up and threw up for real, all the fear and nausea of that day relived over and over and over again.

On the morning of the one-year anniversary of her death, he got up early, packed some gear, dressed Katie in some warm clothes, and set off across the hill on Diamond. They rode and rode back across Clinch River, up Copper Creek on one side, then back down on the other. He took Katie high into the hills and they camped out. She watched him sit on a rock overlooking the Foam Hole at Copper Creek and write his last journal entry:

> I have read and read in my Bible till my head hurts but the words run together now and I can't hear them. I search the pages just like I search old trails in the woods. In the last few days, I've been to the cave, the Hale Springs, even the preacher's barn searching them, too. My arms hang so heavy at my sides like overloaded branches on the apple trees, and my feet are dragging out my tracks. The only words that speak to me now are, "My God, my God, why hast thou forsaken me?"

When Ezra finished writing, he closed the tattered journal, tied it shut with a piece of twine and put it in his knapsack. Katie was chasing a butterfly around, and Ezra caught her by the hand and led her closer to the creek's edge. He took off her shoes and socks and set her down in the edge of the water. Katie let go of his hand and stepped into the muddy ooze, smiling as the water clouded up around her toes. She leaned over to study the little moving blips in the water.

"Tadpoles," Ezra said. "Baby frogs."

"Baby!" Katie said and pinched the water behind the tadpoles with her pudgy little thumb and forefinger. Ezra picked her up, and she started to kick and squeal.

"Come on, we'll get in the water and swim with them." Katie quieted down then and turned serious as Ezra stepped out, carefully testing each stone, the water rising deeper and swifter with each step. Katie clasped her arms tightly around his neck. When the water was about chest high and he had a flat, sandy place to stand, Ezra stopped. He smiled at Katie and splashed a little water up on her shoulder. Then he scooped up a handful and poured it over his face and laughed. She laughed, too. He scooped up another handful and sprinkled it on top of her head.

"I baptize you in the name of—" Ezra paused and listened. He shook his head and started again. "I baptize you in the name of caves, the waterfall, these hills, the stones, and the stars. Now you do me."

He took Katie's little hand, formed it into a cup, and dipped a little water. He directed her hand over to the top of his head. She giggled and reached into the water on her own a second time. Ezra held her there as she dipped and then splashed with both hands, soaking them both, slapping the water harder and harder, the torrents hiding the water that was now falling from Ezra's eyes.

EPILOGUE

Ezra Teague finally did go on with his life. He had to. He eventually married again and fathered eight more children, supporting them by working in the sawmill, farming, opening a little store, and making moonshine. Eventually, he found his faith again and returned to his church. Alma visited his dreams for the rest of his life. He never dreamed of his time in the woods again.

When Ezra was a fairly old man, he heard that the old Wayland Baptist Church was to be torn down so a new one could be built on the same spot. He got up just before daybreak and walked over there. He remembered that he had lain next to a smooth stone to the right of where the pulpit stood. At the church, Ezra struggled through thick blackberry briars, not floating along easily on his feet like he did before. He got down on his knees and looked under the floor. To his amazement, there was the stone, exactly as he remembered it. *Only stone doesn't change, doesn't move, doesn't die,* he thought. Ezra crawled in, lay down, and looked up through the knotholes in the floorboards. The cold earth soaked into his bones as he closed his eyes and heard the exact tone, inflection, emotion in her voice: Ezra Teague.

ABOUT THE
AUTHOR

Rita Sims Quillen's *Hiding Ezra* was a finalist in the 2005 Dana Award competition, and a chapter of the novel is included in *Talking Appalachian*, the recent study of the Appalachian dialect from the University of Kentucky. Rita was one of six semi-finalists for Poet Laureate of Virginia during 2012–2014, and her poetry received Pushcart and Best of the Net nominations in 2012. Rita's most recent collection, *Her Secret Dream*, was named Outstanding Poetry Book of 2008 by the Appalachian Writers Association. Her new poetry chapbook, *Something Solid To Anchor To*, will be published in 2014. Other works by Rita Sims Quillen are the poetry collections *October Dusk* and *Counting the Sums* and a book of essays, *Looking for Native Ground: Contemporary Appalachian Poetry*. Rita lives and farms on Early Autumn Farm in Scott County, Virginia. Contact her on Facebook: www.facebook.com/ritaquillenhidingezra.

ABOUT THE
COVER ARTIST

Willard Gayheart is a celebrated southwest Virginia artist who creates amazing pencil drawings of Appalachian life and culture. A wonderful collection of his work, with commentary, is available via Amazon: *Willard Gayheart, Appalachian Artist.* You can also see and learn more about his work at his website, www.willardgayheart.com.

COMING IN 2014

SOMETHING SOLID
TO ANCHOR TO

NEW POEMS BY
RITA SIMS QUILLEN